The Wayfarer's Inn

The Wayfarer's Inn

PETER B. UNGER

RESOURCE *Publications* · Eugene, Oregon

THE WAYFARER'S INN

Resource Publications
An Imprint of Wipf and Stock Publishers
199 W. 8th Ave., Suite 3
Eugene, OR 97401

www.wipfandstock.com

PAPERBACK ISBN: 979-8-3852-3481-3
HARDCOVER ISBN: 979-8-3852-3482-0
EBOOK ISBN: 979-8-3852-3483-7

07/11/25

In memory of Donald Seagreaves my best friend
and brother in Christ who taught me
the true meaning of friendship.

Contents

The Broken Road

IT WAS A DARK, cold night. The full moon peered out from between the illuminated cloud cover like a celestial eye. As predicted, a snowstorm had begun a short time earlier. The softly, silently falling snow was clearly visible in the glaring headlights of the police cars converging on the scene of the catastrophic accident. It happened on a Friday night on a lonely stretch of highway around 9:00 p.m. The wailing of ambulances could be heard in the distance as they rushed to the scene. Two officers were combing the mangled wreckage for survivors. Two other officers standing to one side shared first impressions. "The tractor-trailer and minibus must have been traveling over the sixty-five-mile-an-hour speed limit judging by the tire tracks and where they ended up after the collision." His partner looking over at the mangled wreck of the minibus remarked in a solemn voice, "It's doubtful there were survivors." The minibus had flipped onto its side and lay across the road perpendicular to the roadside, and extended onto the shoulder of the highway, a twisted, almost indistinguishable mass of metal parts. Ambulances were now on the scene. The driver of the tractor-trailer sustained only minor injuries, a mild concussion as well as scrapes and bruises. Fire police were waving rubbernecking traffic around the safety cones set up around the crash. Further investigation, and the testimony of the truck driver, would reveal that the tractor-trailer had been traveling slightly over the speed limit, around seventy miles per hour. Given the evidence of the truck's tire tread marks and the testimony of the driver it later became clear that he had crossed into the other lane after momentarily falling asleep.

The official report was to reveal that the minibus occupants had been members of a church's governing committee on their way to a retreat center when the crash occurred. Later the state police captain, reading the accident report at a nearby state police station, shook his head and thought to himself how ironic, a church governing committee normally consisting of six elders, six deacons, the pastor, and of course the bus driver. "Well by now they're hopefully holding their retreat in heaven," he remarked to the officer standing in front of his desk, who had brought the report to him. "Perhaps," the officer said, "but I once served on a church governing committee, and I will never do it again, a lot of church politics, and infighting, at least on that one. The pastor confided in me that the only time he drank was after one of those meetings. Once home he made himself a stiff drink, and then vented to his wife while they sat together on the couch."

Pastor Jim had been jarred awake by a cacophony of horrible sounds his brain did not have time to process. He would relive them again and again, those nightmarish flashes of memories and sense impressions; screeching tires, the truck's rapidly approaching glaring headlights, the terrifying anticipation of the impact, and the sensation of being thrown violently forward. Then in an instant he found himself floating in a pitch-black darkness, but instead of feeling panicked he felt an incongruent and extraordinary sense of calm. Slowly as the darkness gave way, he felt himself being gently lowered down and positioned upright until his feet felt solid ground. He then found himself walking, really stumbling forward at first, on what he could now clearly see was an isolated, country road.

Among his first recollections of walking alone on this desolate road, in the dead of winter, were of the steady snowfall and an occasional gust of wind blowing a swirl of snow into his face. As his senses adjusted to this new, strange, mysterious, prairie landscape, he tried to make sense of where he was, and more importantly how he had gotten there. The gravel dirt road had frozen solid and stretched into the horizon, or at least as far as he could see. He could not make out any lights in the distance that might offer hope that a village, a town, or any other sign of civilization lay ahead. A full moon overhead bathed the rural landscape in a luminescent light. A layer of snow and ice covered the fields that lay on either side of the road with both sides gradually stretching off into the darkness. Small thickets of scrub-grass poked out sporadically in places across the fields. Not knowing what else to do, Jim kept walking, hoping he would wake up from whatever this was, a dream or, with trepidation recalling the crash, a coma. And yet it certainly did not seem like any dream he'd ever had. His senses seemed sharper than normal. There was a hyper reality to the whole experience. As he walked on, the snowfall picked up, as did the gusts of wind. Snow drifts began to appear in front of him, half obscuring the road frozen solid beneath his feet. The wind was now continually blowing the swirling columns of snow in his face, making it difficult to see more than six feet in front of him. He zipped up his blue winter parka as far as it would go until it formed a collar around his neck. Jim had no hat and so he periodically dusted the snow off the top of his head and wiped it from his face. While Jim could feel the cold and the way the wind was blowing, he was surprised he didn't feel chilled to the bone. Despite the strange, mystifying experience he was having, he was also amazed that he wasn't panicking. The strange calm he had experienced while floating in the darkness had carried over to his journey down this seemingly endless road. As Pastor Jim continued walking he couldn't help but wonder if he and the others had died in the crash. Was this a near death experience? If so, as a pastor that didn't bode well for him. Where was the tunnel, the bright light, the overwhelming feeling of unconditional love, angelic beings, the life review? There was none of that here. Other questions came to mind. If he had died, had there been any survivors of the bus crash? Jim kept pushing his legs through the deepening snow. The snowdrifts obscured the road in many places, partially blocking his way. He continued to feel strangely calm despite the bizarre circumstances he now found himself in. This, coupled with a strong intuition that this experience had spiritual import, implausibly led Jim to become lost in thought as he plodded on. Troubling thoughts soon came to mind. If he had died in the crash, why had he found himself on this road all alone? Why would a loving God not just take him, doubts and all, and welcome him into His heavenly arms? Could this be a kind of hell, especially if the storm, the road, and his journey were endless? Perhaps the God he thought he knew was not a loving God after all, but the judgmental, patriarchal Old Testament God that some members of his church still believed in, members he had often clashed with over this anthropomorphized belief. Pastor Jim had tried to convince them through sermons, Bible studies, and during visits, that the Scriptures could be seen not as God changing, and evolving, but rather as our human consciousness evolving in spiritually, religiously, and culturally informed ways. This in turn made us better able to receive God's revelations and interpret them, God's progressive covenants with His/Her people being one measure of this.

In seminary Jim came to believe there might be a historical basis for many biblical stories, although he was more doubtful of those in the Old Testament. What many, however, saw as the hand of God working supernaturally in people's lives Jim had come to see as attributable to an ignorance of some purely natural phenomenon. He also had come to regard many authors of Scripture, especially the Old Testament, as having been influenced by their ancient world views which in turn shaped their interpretations of earlier oral traditions. More recently as a pastor preparing sermons, often to his surprise, he had found hidden layers of meaning in many Old Testament texts that bore compelling relevance and meaning for the lives of his parishioners. They also hinted, for Jim, at the overall coherent and synchronous nature of Scripture, the overall composition by its many authors and parts seemingly overseen and woven together by an unseen higher power. He had tried to dismiss this as an after the fact, faith-based reading of Scripture. Still, given the vast span of historical and cultural shifts its pages witnessed to, and the multitude of disparate authors' agendas, Pastor Jim had not found this entirely plausible.

Despite his doubts Pastor Jim had tried to reassure his parishioners that they could still value the transcendent wisdom and overall coherence that shone through all of Scripture, even if only in a metaphorical way. He had tried weaning them away, through sermons and Bible studies, from overly literalistic, and naive Scriptural understandings.

Pastor Jim had most often been met with either indifference or defensiveness from these members. He suspected that this masked an unreflective fear that such new understandings would undermine cherished childhood faith understandings, while suppressing doubts Jim was sure they also had. Even those on his governing committee who seldom cited Scripture, when pressed, would share understandings of Scripture unchanged since childhood. Jim had assured them, and the congregation, that in the long run being open to new understandings might help preserve their faith by allowing it to breathe and grow. He secretly worried that what many of his members were defending were not scriptural understandings built upon a living faith. Rather it was their semi-unconscious reactionary denial that many of their naive understandings of Scripture had been undermined and even broken by an encroaching secular culture pervaded by the modern scientific world and the cynicism of the burgeoning postmodern era. Consequently, the faith that they clung to had been robbed of much vitality and relevance to the times they lived in. Their understandings for the most part were unchanged from their Sunday School years except for the doubts that shadowed their dormant faith lives.

Jim had also tried to reach the congregation through both sermons and Bible studies, with metaphorical interpretations of many key Scripture texts, to help them detach from their non-discriminating literalism, but they had responded with more defensiveness. They had been repulsed by sermons where he clearly was suspicious of and did not affirm the validity of any supernatural occurrences in Scripture, particularly those in the New Testament pertaining to Christ's incarnation and resurrection. Jim's attempts to bring them on board with his overly empirical and rational approach to interpreting Scripture had all been to no avail.

Jim's parents had modeled their faith life for their children. His parents combined a strange mix of Christian beliefs. They leaned conservative in their theological and scriptural beliefs, while remaining more open minded and liberal on social issues. They believed that it was first and foremost Christian love, even when expressed in constructively critical ways, that should be what most characterized one's relationships with others. Both now retired—his father had been a college professor, his mother a counselor—his parents had instilled in Jim and his sister an intellectual curiosity. They had also left the children free to ask questions and share doubts about their faith, and many other things, all through their childhood and young adulthood. Jim treasured this freedom along with the family values his parents had instilled in him. Later, in college and beyond, though, he couldn't help but wonder if the freedom his parents had fostered within him to question his faith had not also nurtured in him a tendency to overly intellectualize it and seek rationalizations to counter faith doubts as they arose. Or perhaps, he thought, this obsessive tendency was due more to an encroaching, secular culture that threatened both the church and faith, his included. Or perhaps it was just his overly analytical nature combined with some mix of the others. Encouraging self-reflection in a young adult, he thought, had to be a good thing, but he was not so sure if his obsession with having to rationally justify his faith to keep faith doubts at bay was such a good thing.

Jim had still chosen to go to seminary after college, as his compromised faith continued to offer him some consolation; the lingering, but diminished hope, meaning, and purpose that his vestige of a faith still afforded him. He had chosen a liberal seminary to avail himself of top-notch scholars in multiple fields from biblical studies to theology to philosophy. The objective scholarly approach of some of his instructors would raise new and troubling questions for Jim while further undermining the somewhat fragile semi-literalistic faith he had entered seminary with.

After seminary Jim accepted a call to his first church of 150 members. Sunday attendance rarely exceeded fifty except at Christmas and Easter. Fortunately, the congregation was content to remain small and forced no unrealistic expectations on him to grow the church. After four years of try-ing to live off the meager salary Jim decided it was time to move on. His next call was to a church of some three hundred plus members, at least on the rolls, whose average attendance on Sundays was around 120. Jim had not heeded the subtle warnings shared as cryptic remarks by members of the search committee such as "we are open to your leadership as long as you respect our most important traditions," and "all we expect you to do is to perform your pastoral duties; we'll take care of the administrative end of things." Jim wanted to accept this call badly. No longer having to preach to a dwindling, small congregation scattered about the pews appealed to him, as did the much better compensation package; and while he hated to admit it, so did the status of pastoring a larger, well-established church in the community. Therefore, he had also downplayed more specific remarks referring to the various sacred cows and cherished long standing institu-tional traditions.

Jim was soon to find out that these so-called sacred cows referred to a broad spectrum of institutional overinvestments among which were the building, social traditions, finances, traditional liturgies, and a variety of other organizational concerns. After a year and a half of receiving a steady stream of negative feedback over nearly every new initiative he attempted to undertake, including the more contemporary liturgies Jim had intro-duced into worship, Jim's patience was wearing thin. Clashes between the different cliques in the congregation over which institutional investments should be given priority were increasing. This had led to worsening ten-sions between both congregants and the governing committee members, which had resulted in face-to-face confrontations and behind the scenes backbiting. Jim's temper had gotten away from him a number of times dur-ing his second year at the church.

On one occasion early on in his ministry several committee members at a meeting had cautioned him not to weigh in on church administrative matters. Clearly annoyed and with his voice somewhat raised, he reminded them in an uncompromising tone that he would be weighing in on ad-ministrative matters, and if this was contested further he would involve the regional hierarchy. Then in a calmer voice he instructed them that administrative matters can impact the spiritual life of the church, and as the spiritual leader of the church it was part of his call as pastor to weigh in on administrative matters. On another occasion a majority of the governing committee, persuaded by a few of its more vocal members, voted against a fundraiser being held at the church. As proposed by Lynn, a committee member, it was to have been for a young family, the parents and two children, who had lost everything they owned when the house they were renting burned down. The fundraiser, through donations and funds raised, was to help supply them with essentials and temporary housing expenses. What precipitated his outburst was a motion made by one of these members, later at that same meeting, to spend a sizable amount, in excess of the building committee's budget, on projects that were clearly not of immediate necessity. Jim had castigated the committee on their misplaced priorities both as Christians and as lay leaders. When met by most with silent indifference he had angrily blurted out, "How can you in any way call yourselves Christians." This incident, which had happened in the early fall of the year, had led him to consider planning a spiritual visioning retreat for the committee that they could then share with the congregation on a Sunday morning in the early new year. This was an idea which he remained tentative on, anticipating much resistance.

A week before Thanksgiving and with Advent fast approaching and with Christmas and the Christmas Eve service a little over a month away, and feeling he had little to lose, Pastor Jim threw caution to the wind and began to plan the retreat. Conflict was tearing the governing committee apart and had long since spilled over into the greater membership where members were choosing up sides, often cliques to which they already belonged. One committee member, who had joined the church only a year earlier, had gone off the committee, and left the church due to the increasing tension and conflict. Short one deacon while retaining the six elders, this left eleven committee members. Personally, Jim felt little motivation to begin planning the Christmas Eve service, and even less interest in selecting the text or theme he would be preaching on, on this Christian high holiday. The fact that there would be visiting extended family members, as well as guests from the greater community, swelling the ranks that night no longer appealed to the side of him that had once relished the attention of such a captive audience.

Jim knew he was a fraud and had largely lost any sense of a legitimate call to ministry. Every time he climbed into the pulpit, he now felt that way. Relying almost exclusively on metaphorical interpretation in his sermons no longer brought him, or his congregants, any comfort. The retreat might not solve anything, but at least he was doing something, taking some action, and even if it hadn't been motivated by a genuine or passionate faith perhaps the Holy Spirit could still work through it somehow. After all, hadn't the disciple Thomas, he reassured himself, continued to follow Jesus to the cross even amid his faith-stifling doubts. It hadn't been easy cajoling the committee members into going on the retreat, but despite their ambivalence, hemming and hawing, and a few decision reversals, Pastor Jim had finally gotten them all on board. The retreat had been scheduled over two days, a Friday and Saturday, on the second weekend before Christmas. A minibus that held up to twenty-five had been reserved to take them to the retreat center, a former convent turned into an ecumenical retreat center still run and maintained by the nuns.

Now with his first-year honeymoon period over at the church, Jim began to have doubts about where he stood with both the committee and the greater congregation. In recent months he had been cold-shouldered by much of the choir, several of whom served on the worship committee, as well as by a few governing committee members. Given that most of these disgruntled members counted extended family members among the greater congregation did not bode well for him either. Not sure if he was merely being overly sensitive and only imagining at least some of this behavior ate away at him. Jim found what he strongly suspected was passive aggressive behavior, hard to combat and nearly impossible to resolve. He had even gone to the home of one influential member of the choir to politely confront her about the palpable tension he sensed between them. She had met him at the door, and with a pensive, aloof manner invited him in. Once both were seated, and the opportune time presented itself, he asked her if there was a problem between the two of them. When she coolly replied, "Not that I am aware of," he responded with a dejected acquiescence. "Then I guess the problem is mine." Given the church's extensive network of grapevines and alliances, he had begun to wonder if his time at the church was now limited.

After walking for what seemed like a long time, and as such recollections and reflections had streamed through Jim's mind, he was once again amazed that he had been able to have such an inner dialogue given the bizarre and the mysterious nature of the experience he was having. He continued feeling the strange calm he had felt from the moment he found himself walking down this mysterious, desolate road. There was an overall ambience about this strange experience that called forth such recollections and reflections in him. Jim leaned into the blustery winter storm and continued shuffling his legs through deepening snow drifts as wind gusts whipped at his face. The snow blowing and spiraling around him only allowed him to see a few feet ahead.

Jim found it increasingly hard to push through deepening snow drifts that were now two to three feet high. He momentarily focused his full attention on the storm raging around him. Then just as quickly he became lost in thought again. More relevant questions came to the fore. "Where am I headed? I may not be freezing to death, or exhausted yet, but I have not seen anything on this road that would give me hope that I will come upon a building, or town. I am beginning to believe this road is endless." For an instant Jim felt a panic arise within him. "What if this is a kind of hell, a hell meant just for me, for one who was always on a spiritual journey without ever having been able to make a faith commitment to a relationship with the Lord, or trust God with his doubts?" It then occurred to him that maybe surrendering these questions and doubts might be the first critical step toward that faith commitment. He also reassured himself that the God of love he knew in Jesus Christ, the Good Shepherd of the sheep who had sought out the one lost sheep, would not give up on him so easily. Maybe this experience did have a purpose he could not yet comprehend. "Maybe," Jim thought, attempting to further reassure himself that if he was in a kind of purgatory and he cried out to God, the God he knew in Jesus Christ would still reach out and save him. Despite the ongoing doubts that plagued him, Jim then reassured himself that he was an essentially good person, who tried to accept his part in conflicts and always tried to reconcile with others.

He knew, particularly as he had increasingly had to confront and deal with the conflicts and hypocrisies in his church, that his faith doubts had only grown and like weeds overcoming the flowers in a garden were choking out what little faith remained. He hated the theological and biblical hairsplitting that had led to centuries of persecutions and religious wars, often due as much to corrupting political and cultural factors as religious differences. None of this was consistent with the most essential teachings and mission of Jesus Christ. A rigid intolerance of divergent Christian belief, born of enshrined institutionalism, over such issues as how God bestows his Grace, the role of clergy, and the hierarchical nature of the church, among many other issues, had over the centuries increasingly created sectarian division. Sadly, such issues were still dividing Christians to this day, albeit in concert with a phenomenon unique to our time, the growing defection, among former churchgoers and their children, to those of the unchurched and noninstitutional Christian ranks. Their weariness and indifference to what they regarded as antiquated religious institutionalism being one major catalyst.

Apathy and desperation over the unceasing conflict in the church had led him to plan this governing committee retreat at the former convent that now welcomed individuals and groups from other Christian traditions seeking a spiritual retreat. His regional hierarchy had recommended a format, one that utilized prayer, devotion, and Bible study, with the goal of formulating a shared spiritual vision. While Jim saw nothing wrong with this agenda, he doubted whether he or his committee members had the faith, understanding, investments, and consequently motivation to take such a retreat seriously. Jim shivered as he felt, for the first time, the blustering wind of the snowstorm chill him to the bone. It momentarily jarred him out of his reflections. He once more resolved to focus solely on moving forward, hoping it would either lead to some destination or come to another comprehensible conclusion. Again, this resolve would not last long.

Jim hunched his shoulders and leaned into the gusting snowstorm, steeling himself to continue this bizarre journey. Later it would occur to him that this journey offered a concrete illustration of the aimless, despairing, isolated, lonely, and exhausting spiritual journey he had been on for so long in his life and ministry. Confronting the harsh reality of his own wayward journey, he thought, why had he held out any hope that his leadership on this retreat would help facilitate a greater spiritual vision for his committee members. Neither were the committee members any more prepared to help formulate any greater spiritual vision of what their church could be. Besides, to get them on board with the retreat agenda, he had disingenuously promised some members that they could raise their respective institutional concerns for consideration in the process of developing a new spiritual vision for the church. He knew of course that this had the potential to obscure and derail any discussion that might lead to a deeper shared spiritual vision. Jim knew as well that even if some of his committee members had ever sought to passionately live out their faith, this had long since been superseded by a worship of the institutional church, their efforts increasingly focused on preserving the church building and organization.

With a wary eye cast toward any newcomers that might threaten such investments they could, if necessary, then circle the wagons around them.

He could not help but wonder if another pastor, whose faith was not so riven with doubts, and lacking in faith-driven passion, would make much headway with this crew. Or perhaps, given the unreflective nature of his members' idolatrous institutional investments, such passion and sermonic integrity would precipitate an even more premature pastoral exit. No, churches like this, Jim thought to himself, needed pastors who did not like to make waves and were content to fulfill their teaching, preaching, and pastoral care duties, while abdicating any greater spiritual leadership role. Deep down Jim knew this was an overly cynical view.

As he shuffled forward amid the current mystifying circumstances his body gradually grew numb, and it was all he could do to keep pushing himself through the blizzard raging around him. Jim was finding it increasingly difficult to push his legs through deepening snow drifts that covered and obscured the road in front of him.

The pale moon in the dark winter sky now offered only a fading light upon the road ahead. Neither could he see the fields anymore on either side of the road. He could barely see three feet in front of him now. An increasing sense of despair was gradually replacing the calm he had felt before. Then, in a moment of utter exhaustion and overcome by feelings of hopelessness and despair, that broke through the remaining calm, he came to an abrupt stop and uttered what, for him, was a most inarticulate prayer. "Lord, I don't know if you're listening, I am not even sure if you're up there, out there, or within me. I don't know why I am on this journey, if it has a purpose, or is even connected to you, but I am lost, alone, and exhausted. Forgive me my doubts, but if you're there please save me from whatever this is." It had not been a well-worded prayer, nor had it been devoid of doubt. Part of Jim still worried, despite the hyper-realism of this experience, if it was all simply the consequence of a traumatic brain injury as he lay dying in a coma in a hospital somewhere, or a prolonged near death experience. Still, the impulse to pray born of a desperate hopelessness had led him, if only momentarily, and perhaps for the first time in his life, to surrender all, including his doubts, to the Lord in prayer. Later as he thought back on it he summed the feeling that came over him succinctly as "screw it all, I am going to trust the Lord to save me at this time."

The prayer offered something of a catharsis. Once more Jim hunched his shoulders and, leaning forward into the wind and snow, he continued the journey. The snowdrifts were so high on the road now, and he had grown so weary, that he had to lift with every ounce of strength remaining first one leg, then the other, to get through the waist high snow. A nightmarish fear flooded over him. What if I am in a vegetative coma and don't die, what if this dream, or whatever it is, goes on and on, at least until my brain totally shuts down? And again, he worried that he might already be dead and in a kind of hell. This journey might then go on forever. Perhaps hell is more like an icy cold, raging winter storm that eventually freezes us in place, making further progress impossible and resulting in spiritual death, than it is the proverbial fires so often imagined.

Letting this horrific imagining subside, he refocused on the present moment and once more chose, in silent prayer, to surrender all, body, mind, and soul, to the God he knew in Jesus Christ.

Jim was now more frequently having to wipe the snow off his head and away from his eyes. He stopped momentarily to catch his breath, and straining his eyes to see through the wind and snow he hoped against hope that he might glimpse a light or the outline of some dwelling place. His heart sank, as he still was unable to see more than a few feet in front of him as the swirling snow blew around him. Just then the name of a country song, "The Broken Road," came to mind. While Jim had always liked country music, among other music genres, and had often listened to it to feel more grounded, the song's title springing to mind at this moment seemed trivial and irrelevant.

Unexpectedly, the wind died down abruptly, and Jim glimpsed a glowing white ball of light in the near distance. Jim's heart leaped with hope and anticipation. Though the wind had momentarily died down, the heavily falling snow still obscured the source of the light. As Jim waded closer, through the waist high snow, all he could make out was a light that appeared to be hovering six or seven feet off the ground just to the right of the road. Exhilarated that he might have found some refuge and respite from this seemingly pointless and increasingly desperate journey, gathering what little energy he had left, Jim, with a quickening pace, pushed through the waist high snow, toward the mysterious light source. Within moments he found himself standing in front of a wooden sign mounted on a wooden post from which a lantern hung. Engraved upon the sign in large letters were the words "The Wayfarer's Inn."

The Inn and Old Pete

THE BUILDING ITSELF WAS a large, one-story log structure nestled in snow that reached halfway up its sides. The full light of the moon had suddenly broken through and revealed a column of smoke curling up and out of a large stone chimney on the middle of the right outer side of the structure. It suddenly occurred to Jim that stumbling upon this inn may have been an answer to his desperate prayer only moments earlier. If so, he wondered, what awaited him upon entry? He approached the large door made from four or five vertical wooden planks with three bolted-on iron plates stretching horizontally near its top and across its midsection and bottom. A large iron ring hanging on its left side provided the means to open the door. Kicking away the snow that had piled up around the front of the door, Jim slowly pulled the heavy wooden door open. While feeling immense relief, and overjoyed that he had finally found a place to rest and recover from his journey, a feeling of anxious anticipation came over him. As the door swung open it revealed two flights of stairs, one leading up into silent darkness, the other down into a basement area. Jim could see that this basement area had a flight of seven steps that led down to a midway landing and then descended the same number down into a well-lit room, where he overheard voices talking in a cheerful, boisterous way. Grasping the knotted rope hanging on the inside of the door, Jim pulled it closed behind him.

He drew a sharp breath in and descended both flights of stairs. Jim paused as he came to the last step and a basement tavern room came fully into view. On his descent he had noticed the iron framed glass lanterns affixed to the squared off posts that the ends of the wooden railings were attached to. The flames of two thick, red candles flickered within the lanterns.

They had a spiral of green ribbon wrapped around them, and offered a warm, decorative illuminating entryway.

What he had seen as he lowered his head beneath the wooden header beam over the stairs astounded him and took his breath away for a second. With a few strangers scattered among them he could clearly see his eleven committee members sitting around the large basement tavern of the inn. Upon seeing Jim, they greeted him with a hearty welcome. "It's Jim," one member cried out. Others immediately chimed in "thank God, Pastor Jim is here." He had not seen such a cheerful harmony among the committee before. It would not last. Another voice Jim did not recognize then boomed out. Although he did not recognize its owner, it too was full of warmth and welcome, its rich baritone timber conveying an air of benevolent authority. Jim turned to see who it was. Behind the bar counter stood a large, broad-shouldered man, bald except for the white hair around the sides and back of his head. The man smiled in a warm, welcoming way and spoke again. "Welcome, Jim, we have been expecting you," he said as he continued wiping out a large pewter tankard with a bar towel. Jim nodded cordially in his direction while wearing a quizzical expression on his face. Another voice then called out to him. It came from a table in the middle of the room. He recognized the voice as that of Williard, who often had an overly friendly way about him. "Pastor, you should sit at the head table," he called out cheerfully. Two of the officers, the president and vice president of the committee, were sitting together at this table directly in front of the fireplace, within which was a roaring and crackling fire. Slightly annoyed by Williard's insistence on protocol given the unusual, to say the least, circumstances they all found themselves in, Jim only half acknowledged Williard's invitation with a slight, impatient nod. He then took a few moments to look around the tavern before slowly making his way over to the table where Scott, the president, and Clark, the vice president, were seated. Alice, the secretary, and Wes, the head of the property committee, were sitting at an adjacent table with Williard. It was at this point with a prearranged nod that old Pete signaled the small group of those staying over from a previous party to take their leave. As they said their goodbyes and exited, they extended their best wishes to the newly arrived committee members, who remained seated.

While smiling and acknowledging his host and the seated committee members, Jim continued for a few moments longer to look about the large basement tavern. His first overall impression was that it appeared inviting and cozy. All decked out with Christmas decorations, it glowed with

Christmas warmth and cheer. It recalled an early nineteenth-century country tavern at Christmas time. His committee members in turn reminded him of the small-town local folk that frequented such taverns, where all knew one another and thoroughly enjoyed each other's company as with a large extended family gathering. The fleeting thought entered Jim's mind that this is what church fellowship gatherings, at their best, without the overimbibing, should be like but so often aren't—a warm, welcoming place full of friends and refreshment: a place of refuge where even a newcomer might experience a sense of acceptance and belonging. Along the back wall of the room a flight of stairs led up to the main floor. Greenery wound around the railing on the right side of the stairs all the way up to the first floor of the tavern. A wooden sign mounted on the wall at the base of the stairs contained an arrow that pointed toward the stairs and read "lodging for overnight guests."

As Jim slowly wound his way around the tables to his seat he continued to take in his surroundings. At the back left end of the tavern, a few feet from the far end of the bar counter, was a door on which a sign hung that read simply in large print "Staff Only." Wooden logs with faded gray-white caulking between them covered the four sides of the room. The ceiling was supported by wooden beams that ran horizontally across the room interspersed by white plaster. The floor was made up of interconnecting flagstones that had been expertly pointed and fit together. Round, wooden tables set about the room consisted of thick planks of conjoined wood. Each table had three or more four-legged wooden chairs around them. A single long, red candle wrapped in a spiral of green ribbon spiked onto a circular pewter candle holder with a curved handle sat in the center of each table. A large pewter pitcher sat on each table, presumably full of beer, as well as a large yet uncut loaf of bread that sat on a wooden cutting board, a bread knife lying next to it. Overhead in the center of the room hung a giant circular iron chandelier. Twelve red candles, also with green ribbons spiraling around them, sat in the iron candle holders affixed at intervals to the edges of the chandelier. Greenery had been wrapped around and in between the large, flickering candles on the chandelier.

Jim had glanced over toward the bar and noticed seven or eight three-legged wooden stools. Their seats had been made from one thick, solid, rounded piece of wood. The front of the bar was covered with conjoined wooden planks, but the counter itself seemed to be made from one massive, rounded board that had a worn, varnished appearance, he guessed from wipe and wear. Greenery ran the full length of the front of the counter and just underneath the edge of the countertop. At the end of the bar counter nearest the entry sat yet another red candle. It too had a spiraling green ribbon wrapped around it. Next to the candle sat a very large leather-bound book on an ornate, intricately carved wooden book stand. The book appeared to be open midway with a white ribbon book marker running down the seam separating the two pages. Jim then noticed a wooden plaque hanging by two short brass chains just beneath the book from the edge of the bar counter with the Scripture verse John 5:39 inscribed on it. Although Jim often could not remember even key Scripture verses word for word, this time at least the exact words of the verse came quickly and clearly to mind: "You study the Scriptures diligently because you think that in them you have eternal life. These are the very Scriptures that testify about me." Jim puzzled for a moment over what this might mean for the governing committee members and him. Jim's eye had then been caught by the floor to ceiling Christmas tree that sat in the far-right back corner furthest from the bar counter. It had been fully decorated with beautiful, multicolored, old-fashioned Christmas balls hanging from its branches. Strings of cranberry garlands and strands of colored Christmas lights wound about the tree, giving it a warm, glowing, luminescent Christmas appearance.

An elongated eight-pointed star had been placed above the tree. It seemed to Jim as though his eyes were playing tricks on him for as he had looked up at it, for a moment at least, a glowing light originating from the center of the star cast out a golden white stream of light toward the mantel of the fireplace before quickly receding. As he approached the table, he felt the warmth of the roaring fire. The stack of logs in the large stone fireplace glowed blue at their center while flames of red and white danced around its edges. A long layer of cotton stretched across the fireplace mantel upon which an assortment of beautifully carved olive wood nativity figures had been carefully laid out. Wise men and shepherds with their flocks adorned either end with a wooden cave stable containing Mary and Joseph and the Christ child occupying the center of the mantel. A large framed cloth, mounted on the wall over the mantel, contained the embroidered words "Home is where heart and love dwell together in faith and grace." While these were quick and fleeting impressions, Jim somehow knew he would be able to recall them. Once again, he was reminded of a cozy, rural early nineteenth-century tavern all decked out for Christmas. Overall, the room's ambience left him with a warm, welcoming, safe, homey, and strangely, given the tavern setting, greater and more spiritual appreciation of the spirit of Christmas. These impressions were yet to be informed by the experiences he was about to have at The Wayfarer's Inn.

Those at the table welcomed Jim once more as he sat down. Williard eagerly approached the head table and, reaching for the pewter pitcher at the center of the table, filled Jim's mug. "The bartender told us," Williard informed Jim as he filled the large tankard, "when we first arrived that the pitchers were filled with a special Wayfarer's beer. No matter how much you drink it doesn't intoxicate. The beer tastes a bit different to each of us. Mine tastes a lot like Guinness Stout, which I happen to love." Williard rambled on, "And it quenches one's thirst wonderfully, and leaves us feeling strangely uplifted, inspired, and more reflective than usual. Audrey of course abstained saying that good Christians don't imbibe spirits." Audrey, under her breath, then added, "Neither should anyone who calls themself a Christian set foot in places like this, which makes me wonder where we really are." Ben paused and glanced over at her. "Audrey, you mean you might be in hell with us. How could that possibly be?" his voice dripping with sarcasm. He then turned back toward Jim and added to what Williard had just said. "I have to say the bread is delicious and quite filling and seems to have a similar effect as the beer."

At this point the bartender, who was wiping out a tankard with a bar towel, paused and spoke. "From here on you can refer to me as Old Pete. The innkeeper asked me to welcome you here." Turning to acknowledge what Old Pete had just said, Scott, the committee president, responded in a self-important and impatient tone. "Old Pete, we appreciate your hospitable welcome to this wonderful tavern, but can you please tell us why we're here, and exactly what this place is all about?" Taking a few moments to respond, the bartender finished wiping out the tankard and then calmly and quietly set it down on the counter. Leaning forward with both arms extended and his hands gripping the edge of the counter, Old Pete looked out at those seated at the tables in front of him. Without answering Scott's question, he then announced, "Since everyone is now here, let me once again welcome you to The Wayfarer's Inn. We offer refuge and refreshment for weary travelers, and lodgings for those who choose to stay over." "This is all very fine and good," Clark, another committee member, whined, "but please answer Scott's question. After all he is our president and spokesperson." He then added, "And if as we suspect might be the case that we're all dead, why aren't we in heaven already?" "This will all become clearer in time, my friend," Old Pete said in a patient but firm voice. Releasing his grip on the counter and throwing the bar towel over his shoulder, Old Pete then came around from behind the bar at its far end and went to sit on the center stool in front of the bar counter. "You are all here because you need to answer a question, a question that by necessity requires some discussion and deeper reflection by each of you. No one," he continued, "not even the innkeeper, can answer this question for you." "What question could that possibly be?" another committee member named Wes blurted out. "That question will be put to you by another," Old Pete responded patiently. For now, allow me to check to make sure you are all listed in our guest book." At that Old Pete stood up and walked back around the counter and toward the large, thick, leather-bound book resting in a book holder at the other end of the counter. Putting on a pair of half reading glasses, Old Pete looked down at the left-hand page in front of him. "I am about to call out each of your names in turn. I will also be making some introductory remarks about each of you. I hope that this will shine a little light on why you are here and help prepare you for the discussion to follow. Please understand it is our intention to help you, as much as we can, to arrive at your own insights as to why you're here. Think of us as facilitators: we may guide you toward deeper understandings and insights, but you will always remain free to choose what you will do with those understandings, and insights." "How is it that he knows our names or for that matter knows anything about us, when we haven't given him this info," Wes whispered into Scott's ear. "Who is this man?" Fred, the treasurer of the committee, whispered suspiciously to all those at his table.

"Is Audrey here?" Old Pete called out.

A gray-haired, bespectacled woman responded, "That would be me" with an air of authority and in a no-nonsense way that epitomized the church lady persona she projected. Undeterred, Old Pete continued. "Audrey, I understand you are the head of the church's quilting group." "Yes, that's me," she answered with an air of prideful authority. "Would I also be correct that the mature ladies that make up the quilters' group also double as the church's telephone prayer chain?" "Yes, we handle that as well," Audrey called back with an air of self-importance. Ben, another committee member sitting at the table nearest the door, whispering just loud enough to be overheard, remarked, "Yes, and three quarters of them are stone deaf." Audrey glowered at Ben. "Most of our congregation knows they should call me first with their prayer concerns. I then pass them on to the next lady on our prayer list. If one of our ladies is unreachable, we know to pass it on to the next lady on the list, until we have completed our prayer chain." "They are more illustrative of a grapevine of near-deaf ladies than a prayer chain," Ben could then be overheard whispering to Lynn, who was sitting next to him. At this Audrey clearly took umbrage and scolded Ben. "I heard that and resent it. We are doing the church a great service by lifting up the afflicted in prayer and keeping the greater congregation informed of their ongoing condition." "Like the time Mrs. Hines made a prayer request for her upcoming gallbladder surgery, and by the time the prayer chain was finished your good ladies were praying for the safe delivery of her baby?" Ben had said this out loud while leaning back in his chair and smirking. "We all make mistakes, you should know that better than anyone, Ben." Audrey was alluding to the difficult time Ben had transitioning back to civilian life, which, among other troubles, included a failed marriage and a battle with alcoholism. Ben deflected her barb with another wisecrack. "Don't know if I'd call it a mistake, Audrey, more of a miracle, as Doris and her husband are in their fifties. I am just glad her husband didn't have any heart issues when members back-slapped and congratulated him the following Sunday." Audrey could then be heard huffing. "Our quilters take their tasks very seriously at the church, Ben; your humor is not appreciated. In fact, since taking over as head of the quilters I made sure we stopped eating out monthly. We now have more money in our account than ever and are better able to donate money to the property committee for their projects. As upstanding moral Christians, we should be serious and frugal servants of the Lord, it shouldn't be about fun and games." "You've got part of that right, you certainly don't believe Christians should have fun," Ben sniped back sarcastically. Old Pete had up to this point been listening to their back and forth banter patiently. Finally, when a brief pause presented itself, he concluded Audrey's introduction by asking Audrey, "Would you say then that your greatest passion and motivation as a Christian is living a solemn, morally upstanding life?" "Well," Audrey replied, "I don't know if I would put it exactly that way, but yes, I think that comes close." "Well, Audrey, it is no surprise that your journey brought you here. Welcome to The Wayfarer's Inn."

Old Pete returned to the guest book and looked at the next name on the list. "Clark," Old Pete called out, peering over his reading glasses and then pausing. Ben once again whispered in a way easily overheard, "We call him Clark Kissup." "You are a fairly new member of the church, are you not?" Old Pete persisted. "Yes, sir," Clark responded in a crisp, deferential tone. "You don't have to call me sir, Clark, around here they just call me Old Pete," Old Pete responded. "I was just trying to show my respect, you are obviously a very important man," Clark, a tall, thin, balding man wearing thick, black-framed glasses, replied in an appeasing tone. Side stepping his comment, Old Pete continued. "It is my understanding that you are the vice president of the governing committee and consider yourself a right-hand man to the president." Clark sat up straight in his chair and glanced sideways at Scott, who lowered his head slightly and let out a resigned sigh. "Well, I don't know if I would go that far. When I served our country in the military, I discovered I had a certain talent. I was an aide to an Air Force colonel and found I had an aptitude for such a position. I was by his side most of the time, kept him on time for his appointments, and was always ready to assist him whenever he needed me. He told me numerous times about how much he valued my assistance. Did I mention that I drove him everywhere he needed to go in his requisitioned Jeep? As a reward he let me borrow the Jeep when not needed. During my time in the military, I always volunteered to serve as an aide to the officer in charge, ready to lend support and assistance." "So do you see yourself as having done something like this on the governing committee with Scott, the president?" "Yes, I felt he could use my help, especially since he's a fairly new member and only became president a year ago." Groans could then be heard from the table nearest the door. "Clark, isn't it also true that you were fired from numerous jobs either along with your boss or because some of your bosses just found you annoy-ing?" Lynn asked in a weary, impatient tone. Clark's face turned beet red, but pretending not to hear the comment, he continued, "At our last annual meeting, in his annual report Scott," he then paused and glanced sideways at Scott as if to get permission to proceed. Scott, his head still lowered, nodded slowly with an indifferent weariness. "Well, Scott," Clark said in a burst of prideful enthusiasm, "told everyone assembled that without my as-sistance much of the work he had done as president would have been much harder. You might say I always have his ear. After all, Scott is an important and successful businessman in our community, and we are lucky to have him as our president. He has the necessary experience to make our church successful. I am just glad I can be of assistance to him as vice president," Clark said with feigned humility. "Is there anyone else that you see yourself serving, Clark? Are there other motivations you can think of for serving your church, that instill in you a certain passion?" Old Pete had asked both questions in quick succession. "Other motivations, sir, I mean, Old Pete? I like to think I am serving God at the same time I am assisting Scott. I am not sure I understand the question." "Thank you, Clark, for sharing what you have, your journey has brought you to the right place. Welcome to The Wayfarer's Inn." Old Pete said, concluding his introduction.

Turning once more to the large book on the counter, Old Pete traced his finger down the page to the next name on the list. Peering over his reading glasses he called out, "Where is Lynn?" "I am over here," she responded waving her hand in the air. Sitting at the table nearest the door was a tall, thin young woman with long brown hair, wearing oval, wire-framed glasses on her rather long face. Old Pete continued, "Being in your early thirties, Lynn, you are one of the youngest members of the committee?" "Well, yes, although I don't appreciate my age being announced in front of a group of people."

Old Pete smiled, "Apologies, but compared to me you are very young indeed. Am I correct, Lynn, in assuming you grew up in the church and are a descendant of members who helped found the church?" "Yes, but that's not the reason I am invested in this church," she responded in a shrill and slightly annoyed tone. "Your parents are quite traditional in their views of the church, and politically conservative as well, is that correct?" "Am I being prosecuted here, where is this line of questioning leading?" "Again, my apologies, but I think it might be helpful if others here learned a bit more about you. Despite having known you as you were growing up, they may not understand your personal reasons for what you see as the most important mission of the church, particularly your home church." "I prefer it that way," Lynn said tartly. "I understand," Old Pete responded, "but in the discussion that follows these introductions it might help both the group and you better understand why you hold the views you do. It might also be helpful for you to reflect on why you do as well. Am I also correct that you love fighting on behalf of the poor and marginalized?" "What I love doing is fighting against social injustice, which is even broader than just fighting for the poor and marginalized," Lynn responded in a shrill tone. "I see you have been the head of the mission committee for several years now." Old Pete had said this more as a statement of fact than a question. Still, Lynn, taking advantage of a short pause on Old Pete's part, asserted, "The resolutions voted on at our national church assembly are supposed to be supported and taken up by the local churches. This has not always been the case with our church. I made certain, though, that all those on the mission committee agreed to advertise these causes, especially on Sunday morning, and to procure mission funds for them. We also restarted our annual walk for hunger and support for the local food pantry." The rest of the governing committee members scattered around the room were uncharacteristically quiet and had their heads lowered, their body language displaying a lack of interest and appreciation coupled with weary annoyance. A few groans had been heard when Lynn talked about her frequent mission appeals on Sunday mornings. "I started attending our regional denomination's annual meeting. I also insisted that a couple mission committee members attend with me. I was one of those that spoke out there in support of the mission resolutions about to be voted on," Lynn said with obvious pride. "I've attended those conferences, they're amazing," Ben said, with a mischievous grin on his face. "A lot of those people love to support such mission causes, but if you're with them at a table and try to get to know them, they are not always the friendliest. They can be a little stiff and cliquish." Lynn cast a disapproving glance at Ben. "Maybe so, but at least they have the right priorities and are willing to help the marginalized and less fortunate," Lynn snapped back. "Lynn, you know I support most of these causes too, but I've got to tell you many of these people are mostly motivated by guilt mixed with a kind of elitist superiority complex. They're happy to give money, just don't ask them to give too much of themselves personally. Fortunately for many of them these resolutions involve causes where nothing personal is required. Honestly, I am not sure they're capable of sharing their faith even in tolerant and non-coercive ways. I recall a sister church in Africa we had donated to so that they could purchase more Bibles, a need they had expressed through correspondence. As we exchanged letters with them, we kept each other up to date on our respective churches, and the challenges we both faced. In one letter they wrote back saying that they would be praying for our church's spiritual renewal. That should have been something of a wake-up call," Ben asserted. "That's even more reason, Ben, why we need to keep educating our congregation about the sociological and political roots of social injustice, as we keep promoting these resolutions. If there's any way to teach them what Christ was all about, it's through such efforts," Lynn responded in a more patient tone, not wanting to strain their alliance. "Anyway, at least one Sunday a month throughout the year, and more often around the holidays," Lynn continued, "I promote these mission resolutions at the back of our church. I do my best to ensure that our congregation won't ignore or forget about them."

A few governing committee members sitting at other tables muttered audibly in unison, "You can say that again." "You may not appreciate the mission causes I inform you about," Lynn snapped back, "but I will not let you ignore them." "It's not so much the mission causes, Lynn," Williard said in an appeasing tone, "it's the way you hit us over the head with them. People might be more willing to get on board with some of them if your approach was more, let me find the right word, yes, pleasant. Some people find you a bit scary. I just don't think guilt trips work well Lynn," Williard added in an appeasing but slightly condescending tone. "You mean I should be more like you?" Lynn snapped back with a sharp edge to her voice. "Williard, I don't constantly worry about whether everybody likes me or not like you do. Sometimes it takes an approach like mine just to wake some people up." Then in a calmer tone Lynn added, "The prophets of the Old Testament are a good example of this. I also love what Jesus said in Matthew 6:10, in the Lord's Prayer. It is clear here that Jesus expects us to partner with God to help bring His Kingdom to fruition on earth." With Williard appearing cowed and hurt, Alice, feeling sorry for Williard, offered a halfhearted defense of him. "Williard may try too hard to please everybody but at least he has a better feel for where the congregation is at on these issues than you do, Lynn." "Thanks Alice, I think," Williard mumbled under his breath.

Old Pete then jumped in to get things back on track. "I am aware that there is a lot of tension and conflict on this committee, and that this is reflective of divisions within the greater congregation. I have allowed you to air some of these differences, but you will soon have a chance to have a more in-depth discussion where I hope some of these differences might be taken up more constructively. My main purpose right now is to make these introductions and help prepare you for the discussion that follows. So, Lynn," Old Pete continued, "would you say that supporting social justice issues is what you feel most passionate about as a Christian?" Lynn grew silent and reflective for a few moments as Old Pete waited patiently for her answer. "Yes, I guess so," Lynn stated in a suddenly assertive and confident tone. "As you probably already know, after college I worked for a time in another state as a social worker. When I moved back into the area, the only reason I got re-involved in the church was that it afforded me an opportunity to raise awareness of the social justice resolutions our national church supports, as well as other important social justice issues. I grew up in this church, but in college I began to see how far behind the times, how institutionally entrenched and reactive to the rapidly changing culture our church was. To be honest I stopped attending church after college, and no longer even considered myself a Christian. If not for the opportunity to educate about and fight for social justice, I doubt that I would have rejoined my home church. I guess I still have an emotional investment in this church and hoped as one of their own I might be able to open their eyes to the true mission of the church. Although at times I must admit it seems hopeless." "Well, Lynn," Old Pete remarked in a kind but enigmatic way, "it is no accident that you found your way here. Welcome to The Wayfarer's Inn." At this Lynn sat back feeling as if, without fully understanding why, the wind had just been taken out of her sails.

Old Pete turned his attention back to the book sitting in the holder and once again traced his finger down the page and then called out, "Scott, you are next on my list." Looking up from the book and over his reading glasses Old Pete added, "You are the president of this governing committee, are you not?" Scott, who was leaning forward with his head slightly lowered, forearms resting on his knees, and hands clasped together between them, lifted his head just enough to peer up at Old Pete. He then answered him in a flat-affect, businesslike tone. "Yes, that's correct." "Scott, you are a fairly new member of the church, aren't you?" Old Pete continued. "I've been a member for about three years," Scott responded with a hint of weary impatience creeping into his voice. "Yet after only a couple of years you were asked to serve on the committee, in fact the very next year weren't you approached about being president? Why do you think that was?" Old Pete asked. Clark suddenly sat bolt upright and raised his hand and with a burst of enthusiasm cried out, "I was the head of the nominating committee at that time. Scott was and is a very successful businessman, and with our church divided and our membership in decline, and considering that he built a very successful business, it seemed like the natural choice for our church organization. We thought that if we put him in charge, he could help resolve our conflicts and help us grow. And if you think about it, isn't running a church a lot like running a business?" "Well, that's refreshing. I was getting tired of Fred's football analogies and accompanying jargon when referring to our monthly offertory totals as either a win or a loss," Ben sniped sarcastically. Old Pete peered over his glasses and fixed his gaze on Clark, who was sitting next to Scott, and in a patient but firm voice said, "Thank you, Clark, but the way this works is that each individual must speak for themselves." "Yes sir, I mean, Old Pete," Clark responded and then leaned sideways toward Scott and whispered something in his ear. "You see why he's called the Scott whisperer?" Ben wisecracked. Once more turning his attention back toward Scott, Old Pete asked, "So Scott, why did you feel called to serve on the committee?" Scott hesitated before responding, then sat back in his chair, and with the same slightly weary sigh and impatient manner, as if this whole affair was beneath him, responded, "I believe in giving back to the community and that serving the church is one way to do this." "So," Old Pete followed up, "would you say that this is your foremost passion for serving the church?" "I am not sure passion is the right word, I certainly feel it is my duty to give back." Is there anything you feel passionate about in relation to your serving the church?" Old Pete inquired. "Again," Scott answered, sounding clearly annoyed, "I feel that it is my duty to serve the community. One way I can do this is through the church,so no, I don't feel any great passion about this. I just feel that I am doing the right thing. I was able to build a very successful business and hope to bring this experience to bear as the president of the governing committee, and as Clark said I can't see how running a church as an organization would be that different from running a business." "Thank you, Scott," Old Pete concluded. "It is not by accident that your journey has brought you to The Wayfarer's Inn, welcome."

Old Pete turned back to the large, mysterious, leather-bound book, and once more traced his finger down the list of names. "Williard," Old Pete called out. "I am over here, Old Pete," Williard answered in a way clearly meant to please. "You are a lifelong member who has served the church, at one or another time, as treasurer, secretary, and vice president." Old Pete continued, "You see yourself as a valued mediator who helps keep the peace between differing cliques and individuals in the church, particularly those on the governing committee." "I do," Williard responded, "I know many wouldn't believe this, but churchgoing Christians are all too human." "Really," Old Pete responded. "Do you think that's what many people outside the church believe?" Old Pete quipped in a gently mocking tone, that nonetheless missed its mark. "Oh my, I hope not, and what's more the congregation looks up to us as leaders in the church, and assumes we were picked for our wisdom and maturity." "Strange," Ben wisecracked, sitting back in his chair with a bemused look on his face. "When it comes to the governing committee, I just thought the nominating committee was relieved and happy if they could just fill the slots available." "I've learned not to expect anything positive to come from Ben, he seems to be angry at the world," Williard sniped back in a disingenuously pleasant and condescending tone. "Not the world

Williard, just the leadership of this church." "Whatever, Ben," Williard said. He then deflected the comment by changing the subject. "A couple of the men on the governing committee are Masons and, as most know, to become one requires that established Masons attest to their character. I was invited onto this committee on their recommendation." "So, Williard, have you had to intervene often in church conflicts?" Old Pete interrupted, sidestepping his last statement. "Funny you should ask; we recently had a conflict between two parties on the governing committee over whether to make our church handicap accessible by having a ramp built. I could see both sides of the issue." "Of course you could," Lynn muttered audibly under her breath. Undeterred Williard continued. "I told the side not in favor of spending the money that I got where they were coming from. We only have a few elderly individuals who would use it. Moreover, we were informed by the man who drew up the blueprint for the ramp that given the church's frontage a long ascending stretch would be necessary before the ramp zigzagged back to the front door. Frankly this first part of the ramp would look like a toboggan run and would no doubt be off-putting to our only wheelchair-bound church member, an elderly widow. In wintertime, even if salted, that ramp's bound to get pretty slick. Good heavens, if she ever lost forward momentum and rolled back down that ramp there's no telling how far she'd go. The road out front runs downhill all the way into town." "Williard are you really suggesting she might go whizzing through town?" Ben said in a mocking tone. "There's nothing funny about this, Ben, of course not that far," Williard scolded. His voice, which became even higher pitched when upset, seemed to have climbed a squeaky octave higher. "You implied it, I didn't," Ben responded, reclining back into his chair. His bemused smile showed the pleasure he derived from getting under Williard's skin. Old Pete rubbed his forehead slightly, displaying for the first time a bit of consternation, and appeared ready to intervene when Alice, at the head table, yelled out, "Williard, for heaven's sake finish answering the man's questions so we can move forward with the agenda here, whatever that might be." "Very well," Williard replied in a submissive and hurt tone. "I was also able to empathize with the other side too. I told them I could understand their position as well. They felt that even if only a few members were more easily able to attend the church, the building of the ramp would be justified. They also felt a ramp out front might attract new members." "That would be false advertising," Ben muttered under his breath. Lynn, who was one of those who had argued in favor of building the ramp, nudged him with her elbow and holding a finger to her lips motioned for him to be silent. "And exactly how did this help mediate the conflict?" Old Pete inquired patiently. "Oh, I see your point," Williard answered. "You see, everyone on the committee knows they can come to me anytime and use me as a sounding board, and this of course helps to defuse tension." "So would you say, Williard," Old Pete followed up, wanting to conclude his introduction, "that you have a passion for pleasing people?" "Well, I would word it differently," Williard responded, again appearing a bit wounded. "My passion, and by the way I've heard you use that word several times now, is serving the church as a peacemaker. I provide an outlet for everyone to defuse their anger and feel understood, then they are less likely to vent that anger at those they disagree with. And as I am sure you know Jesus taught that we should always turn the other cheek. I have always understood this to mean that we should never get angry with those we disagree with, especially those of us in Christian leadership." Williard had glanced over at Pastor Jim in a disapproving way as he said this. "Better to vent behind the scenes to someone like me. I see myself as facilitating this in my role as mediator." "Is that what Jesus meant," Old Pete responded in a gently mocking tone that left Williard momentarily confused. "I will concede this," Williard went on as an audible groan arose from a few of the tables, "my wife once remarked to me, 'Has it ever occurred to you that by trying to agree with all sides of a conflict you might be creating more animosity behind the scenes?' But even here I was able to defuse the situation. Utilizing the skill I've gained as a mediator over many years I told her I could see her point, which at the time seemed to reassure her. In any case, with a slight shake of her head, she walked away without saying another word. And one more thing, a lot of our members just want to come to church on Sunday morning and then go home. The last thing they want is an open conflict in our church, so you might say," Williard added, appearing quite pleased with himself, "I am a stand-in for them as well." "Well, Williard," Old Pete said, "we need to move on. Trust me when I tell you that it is no accident that your journey brought you to The Wayfarer's Inn." Williard sat back, looking more than a little befuddled.

Once again Old Pete turned back toward the big leather-bound book and traced his finger down the page. "Debbi," he called out. "I am over here," a heavy-set, well-dressed young woman sitting in the corner of the tavern nearest the Christmas tree called back. She was sitting with her hands folded demurely in her lap. "Debbi, I understand your family goes back some eight generations to the very founding of the church." "Yes, that's correct," Debbi responded, beaming with pride as she sat primly and properly in her chair. "An ancestor of mine was a signer on the church's charter. Is it okay if I say something more?" "Go ahead," Old Pete said. "When I was in confirmation with our previous pastor, he helped me realize what I treasure most about our church. We all loved Pastor Bill. He was the pastor of our church for nearly thirty years," Debbi interjected in a saccharine tone. Pastor Jim slumped back in his chair with a resigned, weary expression, as if he had heard such comments one too many times. He had often wondered if part of the reason he had had so much trouble winning the affections and respect of the congregation was due to the former pastor's long tenure. He had done little to prepare the governing committee or congregation for his departure. Pastor Bill, as they called him, had also developed close friendships with many colleagues. Soon after he started Jim had been informed by a pastoral colleague that he had big shoes to fill. Jim had not only found such comments unhelpful but given their seminary training and ministry experience surprisingly unskillful. Pastor Bill had pastored the church with a benevolent authoritarianism, and his leaving had left a clique of ambitious laity empowered by the power vacuum he left behind. "Anyway," Debbi continued, "Pastor Bill asked our confirmation class to undertake a project that celebrated the history of our church. We were coming up on the one-hundred-and-fiftieth-year anniversary of the church. He asked us to break up into twos or threes and create a variety of historical displays celebrating our church tradition, history, and the culture of the greater community. We were then to put these onto poster boards to be displayed in the back of the church on the Sunday this celebration was to occur. Pastor Bill even gave us ideas, such as a poster board with old pictures from the archives of the church and its members, or alternatively historic pictures of the greater community that included pictures and brief descriptions of some of the different churches in town. He also suggested we could create a timeline of the church's one-hundred-and-fifty-year history. That history might also include significant events in the life of the church and some of the greater community. As an alternative to the poster he suggested we could put together a video of confirmands interviewing some of the oldest members of the church about their earliest memories of the church. Since the families of all three in my group went back to the founders of the church, I thought it would be really neat if we could put together a genealogical chart on poster boards that connected our three families back to charter members of our church. I asked Pastor Bill if this was alright. He appeared a bit hesitant and concerned, but he finally gave us the okay. We already knew that our three families were related." Debbi paused and looked around the room at some of the members of the committee as if needing their approval to continue; most smiled and nodded encouragingly. "And how did that turn out?" Old Pete prodded Turning back toward Old Pete and sidestepping the question, she chirped enthusiastically, "My dad even helped me out with the project. He bought us a number of rectangular poster boards for each of our extended families so we could trace our ancestry back to one or another of the church founders. We saved a couple of these to put over the others where we hoped to connect all three of our family trees back to our three respective founding families."

Debbi then paused, and her expression took on one of disappointed frustration. "Unfortunately, it didn't work exactly as we planned," she said, sighing and frowning. "And why was that Debbi?" Old Pete asked. "Well as it turns out, our families had intermarried more than once across the generations, and this seems to have increased as time went on. To be honest our family trees didn't exactly fork as we had expected." "Well, that explains a lot," Ben muttered under his breath, careful this time not to be overheard beyond those at his table. "Not nice, Ben, my family goes back that far too," Lynn snapped back at him.

Just then Debbi's demeanor changed again and with a burst of youthful exuberance she tried to put a positive spin on the problem. "But I see the multiple inter-relations of our families as a good thing. We tend to stick together on all the important issues facing our church. And I might add," she said with a well-rehearsed laugh, "you have to be very careful about what you say about one of us, as you might end up getting half the church mad at you." The weary, annoyed expression on Pastor Jim's face as he shook his head in quiet dismay clearly indicated that he did not see any humor or positive implications in this and felt such a dynamic contributed to the church's dysfunction. "So, you see that as a good thing?" Old Pete asked. "Yes, I do," Debbi replied without hesitation, "especially when it comes to newcomers wanting to make major changes in our church. Although I hate to admit it, there are those whose families go way back in our church who are also pushing for a lot of changes." As Debbi said this, she cast a scowl across the room in Lynn's direction. Lynn, seeing this and hearing the remark, smiled back derisively. "They say it's time to embrace change and new causes as if they own the place. They forget it was our church long before it was theirs." "Your church?" Old Pete asked with a gentle but puzzled expression. "That's right, our families not only started the church but have maintained it for nearly one hundred and fifty years. I think it's safe to say without us there wouldn't be a church," she huffed with an air of self-satisfaction. "And if you need any more proof, our names are all over the place, on the pews, the stained-glass windows, plaques, you name it. One of our families even donated money for a new communion chalice in memory of their family matriarch; they insisted her name be engraved right across the front of the chalice for all to see every time we celebrate communion. It reads 'In Memory of Gladys Heffelhoffer.' Pastor Jim will attest to that." At this Jim puffed out his cheeks and let out an exasperated, breathy sigh. "I don't think you need any more proof that this was our church long before anyone else's and that we should have more say." "So is it safe to say, Debbi, that for you being a Christian is tied to a strong sense of ownership of the church, that stems from being a lifelong member and descendent of church founders?" Old Pete followed up. "Yes," she replied, bursting with oblivious pride. "Is that what you believe will save the church in the end?" Old Pete then asked. "I do," Debbi responded, her hands still folded neatly in her lap, clueless as to the direction Old Pete's questioning was leading her. "Let me ask you a different question, Debbi, one you may not have considered: What would you say if someone asked you what it means to be saved as a Christian?" Old Pete asked this peering over his reading glasses at Debbi with a concerned but penetrating stare, though not intending to press the matter further. "I don't know if this is a trick question or not, but I have to believe that being a lifelong member of the church would have to be one answer to this question." For the first time Old Pete let out a slightly exasperated sigh. "Well Debbi, let me assure you it is no accident that you find yourself at The Wayfarer's Inn, welcome."

Old Pete turned yet again to the large leather-bound book, and again traced his finger down the list of names. "So, Alice," he began, "I understand that while you grew up in another church in the community when you got married you joined your husband's church." Having said this, Old Pete peered over his reading glasses at Alice, who was sitting at the head table in front of the fireplace. A woman of a medium build in her early sixties, Alice had grayish-white, shoulder-length hair and reading glasses that lay across her chest. They were held in place by a thin metal chain attached to the arms of her glasses, which ran around the back of her head. Upon hearing Old Pete start her introduction she sat up ramrod straight, put on her reading glasses, and stared back at Old Pete intensely. This gave the impression of an old person stare-off as both peered over their reading glasses at each other. "Yes," she replied after a brief pause in a somewhat shrill, businesslike tone, and appearing rather tightly wound. "Many years ago, when I married Bennet I joined his church, but judging by everything I've heard you already knew that and didn't need to read this out of that book," she replied with a sharp, schoolmarmish edge to her voice. Ignoring her comment, and unaffected by her shrill, scolding tone, Old Pete glanced back at the big leather book. "I understand as well that you were the medical manager at a large family practice until retiring a few years ago, and that more recently you have served on both the governing committee and property committees of the church and as the secretary." This time Alice did not respond, but just stared back with a tight-lipped, defiant intensity at Old Pete. Without glancing down at the book, Old Pete then remarked, "And recently haven't you also served as chair of the task force charged with revising the rules and policies regarding the uses of the church? It is my understanding that the revisions here further restricted the use of the facilities not just for any outside groups but for church members as well. Permission forms that clearly outline these changes are now required to be filled out?" "I have no idea where you're going with all this, but so far at least you've got your facts straight," Alice said in a snarky way. Old Pete persisted. "In one of its revisions didn't the committee include stricter guidelines for any mission fundraisers held in the church fellowship hall?" "These rules and policies are so restrictive they not only block misuse of the building by some outside group, but any mission fundraiser, however justified by context and Christian ethical concern," Lynn, in an accusatory tone, interjected. "Remember when we tried to put on a fundraiser at the church for a family who had lost their house and all their belongings in a fire? As I am sure you'll recall you persuaded others on the governing committee that this fundraiser could not be held in the church fellowship hall since neither husband or wife were members of the church." "Calm down Lynn, you're becoming overwrought again," Wes, another property committee member, chided in a patronizing tone. "I bet you say that to all the women who strongly disagree with you, Wes," Lynn snapped back sarcastically, and then followed it with, "I guess it also helps distract from the possibility that you and Alice care more about policies and rules than your fellow human beings." "Now Lynn," Alice responded with a well-practiced tone of self-righteous condescension. "You know very well that it has been the unwritten policy of this church for many years to only allow our facility to be used for a fundraiser on behalf of church members, preferably active ones, and then only within limited parameters. It has also been a long-standing policy of our church to only extend modest monetary assistance to worthy members. We simply formalized these unwritten policies. There are just too many people out there who would otherwise take advantage of the church for all the wrong reasons." "Yes," Fred said, "such as drug addicts, and those who refuse to get a job. Then there's those who'd become members just to get money out of the church." "You're broad brushing all such charitable acts with these paranoid what-ifs," Lynn replied with weary impatience. Then, allowing for a dramatic pause, her tone changed. Speaking loudly, forcefully, and emphasizing every syllable, she stated, "They were a hard-working couple with small children who had just lost everything they had." Then speaking in a calmer, yet businesslike tone she added, "How does this in any way fit the worst-case scenarios you're describing. Context matters," Lynn then said in an angry and exasperated tone. Old Pete, sensing that the contentiousness was escalating, interrupted in a firm voice clearly indicating he was putting an end to the exchanges. "So, Alice," Old Pete said without looking back at the book, "I am gathering that for you staying in control is very important." "Well, I won't deny it, I think maintaining a degree of control is a critical skill to have, be it about running a church or in any other leadership capacity. I think this even extends to maintaining a disciplined control over one's household, for instance where one spouse is better than the other at handling the finances responsibly and efficiently. My husband, Bennet, would be the first to tell you how much he appreciates these aptitudes in me." "I'll say this for the man; he never had to make another decision in his life after he married her," Ben whispered into Lynn's ear. "And it was just as critical when I was a family practice medical manager. I was often praised for the efficiency with which I ran things there. After all, in that setting time was money. I made sure everyone, both doctors and nurses, stuck to their schedules and moved patients along as efficiently as possible." "I think she means as quickly as possible," Ben whispered to Lynn. "After all, time is money," Ben followed up sarcastically.

Old Pete did not respond, he just peered over his reading glasses at her with a sympathetic but concerned look. Feeling increasingly uncomfortable by the second Alice filled the awkward silence, with her shrill schoolmarmish tone, by offering an additional rationale for the imperative of maintaining disciplined control over one's life. "Besides, as I taught my children from little on up, God gave us a reasoning mind and expects us to use it. By temperament I am a very organized, detail-oriented person, so as a church leader I use my God-given reasoning mind and aptitudes. If some see me as being controlling, so be it." "Has the thought ever occurred to you as a Christian, Alice, that prayer might help you resolve problems in a humbler way where you don't always have to be in control?" Lynn shot back. "I don't have a great prayer life myself, but then I don't I have your control issues either. Might also help you to be less tightly wound," Lynn added, conveying a strange mix of empathy and disdain. Dismissing Lynn's advice Alice responded, "I only pray after I have made every effort to solve a problem on my own and was unable to. This hardly ever happens. This is one of the reasons why I keep telling Pastor Jim when he opens our committee meetings with his prayer and devotion to keep it short and sweet. I want to get down to the business of solving our church's problems. I think the infinite God of the universe has better things to do than to be bothered with all our petty problems. Besides, Pastor Bill's prayers and devotions never went more than a few minutes, while Pastor Jim's have been known to drag on for ten minutes or more." At this remark Pastor Jim leaned forward and, placing his elbows on the table, he put his face in his hands and shook his head frustration. Alice, who was sitting at an adjacent table, continued to ignore his increasing displays of frustrated apathy. "So, Alice," Old Pete said, "would it be fair to say that preserving the church building, fueled by a driving need for control, is what best characterizes any passion you might feel for serving the church?" "Well," Alice sputtered, "I think that casts it all in a very negative light. Might I add, and I know Wes agrees with this, as church leaders it is our responsibility to preserve this historic church building so that generations to come may enjoy it." "You may preserve the building," Lynn snapped back, "but there won't be any members left to enjoy it." At this Old Pete interjected, "Alice, I think we can safely assume that your journey led you straight to The Wayfarer's Inn, welcome." As Old Pete said this Alice, recognizing that Old Pete's remark implicated her as much as the others, slumped somewhat petulantly down in her chair and muttered, "Whatever."

Yet again Old Pete returned to the book and traced his finger down the list of names. "Ben, let me turn to you next. It tells me here that while your name is Benjamin, you go by Ben." Ben, a tallish, closely cropped brown-haired, bearded man, in his mid-forties, appeared to have been caught off guard as Old Pete's gaze settled on him. He looked startled and sat up quickly in his chair as Old Pete had called his name. Despite his repeated wisecracks, he was uncomfortable being the center of attention. Ben did not respond but looked back at Old Pete expectantly. "Ben, you've been a member of the governing committee for several years now." Old Pete had posed this as a statement of fact rather than a question. "I have," Ben responded in a quiet, respectful tone. "It is also my understanding you married your first wife, a church member, soon after leaving military service. This marriage did not last. Some years later you married a young woman named Janet to whom you've been happily married for nearly fifteen years now," Old Pete followed up. "This is all true," Ben replied quietly, not sure if an answer was required. "And Ben, is it true that some have questioned whether you should even serve on the governing committee?" "When I first came home from Iraq I battled alcoholism. This contributed to my failed first marriage, a DUI conviction, periods of unemployment, and even a brief period of homelessness. My first wife's family were prominent members of the congregation and due to our breakup ended up leaving the church. Behind the scenes, at the time, gossip among their many good friends in the church presented me in the worst possible light. Some here would still like me to wear a mantle of disgrace that forever ties me to that difficult time of my life. This despite my not having had a drink in many years and having been married to my wonderful wife for as many years, who has since joined our church. Christian forgiveness and reconciliation are apparently not part of their Christian vocabulary. Scott and Audrey also seem unable, or unwilling, to let go of my past and the need to judge me on it. I know what Audrey's issue is, but I am still unclear why Scott, a newer member, is so invested in tearing me down at every opportunity." "Perhaps you will understand each other better as your discussions here progress," Old Pete interjected.

"What I do know is that in committee meetings when I support Lynn's mission initiatives, offer an opinion, or suggest some new initiative Scott consistently uses his position as president to brush me aside or shoot me down. Audrey, I know, values being an upstanding, moral Christian above all else, so at least I know where she's coming from." "You may have served your country with honor, Ben, but you dishonored it by the way you behaved after you came home," Audrey snapped back at him. "I was later diagnosed with PTSD, Audrey; do you even know what that is? So, you see how it is," Ben said, looking back at Old Pete. "I still hear from others, particularly Williard, that some folk in the church still believe I should not be on the governing committee. Williard then commiserates with me, but why don't these folk ever have the courage to come and say this to my face? It hurts my wife as well, and she has suggested numerous times that we join another church. She tells me that the church in which she grew up and most likely many other churches would never treat a veteran this way. But I am stubborn, and perhaps angry enough not to take her advice. I carried a pocket Bible with me in Iraq and read it nearly every day. How, I ask you, is their behavior in any way consistent with what Jesus taught in the Gospels? I don't think any of these people have picked up the Bible and read what Jesus taught and did since childhood, particularly those parts having to do with forgiveness and reconciliation." "I am not against those things, but there are consequences in this world for certain behaviors. In your case I just don't believe you have exhibited the character necessary to serve in a leadership capacity in this church. Past behavior being the best predictor of future behavior," Scott then added. "Maybe I am wrong," Audrey followed up, "but I agree with Scott. I just don't think a leopard can change its spots." Old Pete, having heard enough, stared sternly over his reading glasses first at Scott and then Audrey. "You both have had a turn, so for now let Ben finish."

"And another thing," Ben added, "according to Williard those who talk me down behind the scenes always insist on being anonymous and say they're speaking for a lot of other members. Awhile back I suggested at a governing committee meeting a policy be established that anyone who has a complaint can no longer raise it anonymously, be it about me, other staff, other church leaders, or Pastor Jim. What if it's the same few people or person, or even just Audrey and some of the quilters? Also, such talk is often made to sound like it's half the congregation. Pastor Jim was for this and explained how anonymous complaints could, among other things, foster malicious gossip, something condemned in Ephesians 4:31 and in other places in the New Testament. A few other members including Lynn thought such a policy would help keep us honest, and forthright, and encourage us to share such feedback in more constructive ways, but it got voted down. Williard, while saying he understood where we were coming from, spoke out against it as something that might create all kinds of tension and division in the church and insisted that most of our members just wanted to come to worship on Sundays and then go home. He also argued that if people couldn't remain anonymous nobody would dare come forward to address serious issues that otherwise would go unnoticed. Pastor Jim tried to remind everyone that unresolved conflicts that fester within the congregation had the greater potential to create unbridled tension and division, but it was all to no avail. I know Pastor Jim has also had to deal with critical remarks about him the same way. It all seems backhanded, passive aggressive, and frankly cowardly to me." Ben then paused and shook his head in apparent anger and frustration.

"I am glad you shared all this, Ben. Is there anything more you would like to add before we finish with your introduction?" Old Pete then asked. "Well, there is one more thing, something that also contributes to the anger I feel in relation to this church. I have not shared this with the committee before." A brief pause followed where Ben struggled to control his emotions. He then began to share some of his innermost feelings in a tone that clearly expressed a mixture of hurt and anger. "It's not just the way Scott and Audrey feel about me, it's the example they and others set, the way they talk down to me, and influence others negatively in this way in our church. This encourages them to gossip about me as well. That I've held a succession of what some might consider low status jobs in recent years has become fodder for some of this behind-the-scenes talk. They say I can't hold a job for very long. The fact is I like to stay physically active and have always been a hard worker. I've worked construction jobs and done custodial work. I am currently trying to build up a landscaping business. There isn't much security in some of these jobs, but I've always been able to find another one quickly, and the people I've worked with know that I am a reliable, hard worker. Never cared much for status either. My wife, who's worked as a nurse at a regional hospital for many years, affords a contrast to my work record, which fuels some of the gossip. Janet assures me that it's due to my history with the church that many of these negative dynamics have arisen. But why should I be the one to leave.

"There are certain people in this church that I never seem able to strike up a friendly conversation with, and I can't help but wonder if the behind-the-scenes talk is the reason for this. Perhaps I am being oversensitive about some of this, but I don't think it's all in my head. I sometimes wonder if Jesus came and sat in the back row of our church, like in that famous painting by Holman Hunt, what he would think of us, or us of Him. In the Gospels it was those of low status and reputation that He associated with most." Ben's voice cracked with emotion as he said this, hinting at the depth of anger and disappointment he felt over all the negative experiences he'd had at the church. Clearing his throat and regaining control he added, "I am sure it doesn't sit well either with some in this church that I have gotten behind a number of the mission causes Lynn has pushed for, and have argued with her against some on the governing committee that context and Christian ethical motivations matter as well, if not more than church rules and policies. Well, I've probably said more than I should have, and have certainly shared more than I ever have before with this group." "Thank you, Ben, for honestly sharing these deeper feelings. Risking being vulnerable with this group could not have been easy," Old Pete said empathetically. "My wife says I am gradually turning into an angry, cynical person largely due to what's going on at the church, and as I said before she tells me we should join another church. She may be right, but I also tell myself, given all the negative unchristian-like behavior and conflict going on in this church, maybe this is where the Lord wants me. I am not the most religious person, but at least I know that being a Christian is more than caring about the building and other such institutional investments. It just seems that all that many of our church members and most of our governing committee members care about are the trappings of the church, and not the living faith community it's meant to harbor. They're mistaking the shell of religion for the living spiritual organism of the faith community that should dwell within it. I often wonder and worry that many other overly institutionalized churches in different traditions are becoming like those empty seashells you find on the beach."

"Ben, thank you for sharing these concerns as well, I hope it will give everyone here food for thought. At this time, though, I must ask you the same question I've asked the others: What would you say is your greatest motivation or passion as a Christian in serving the church?" "Well, I have my faith doubts like everybody else. I could be more spiritual, you know, pray more and that kind of thing. Also, as you've probably gathered, I have an anger problem." Then swallowing hard, Ben added, "And if I am totally honest, I could act more out of Christian love, particularly to those I feel resentment toward. In general, like so many in this church, I need to strive with the Lord's help to live out my faith more at home and in my daily life. It's just that I am so angry about what's going on at the church. I figure I'll stick around if only to be a thorn in their side and to expose the hypocrisy and petty idolatry so rampant in our church," Ben added angrily. "So would you say that what most motivates you to stay active as a church member is your anger, then?" Old Pete persisted in a sympathetic but probing way. Ben lowered his head, then slowly lifted it and replied, "I pretty much admitted just that, didn't I," in a tone suggestive of both humility and shame. "Well

Ben, even with the best of intentions and efforts our faith journeys often do not follow a straight course. And in some cases, we might need to let the Spirit awaken us to the hurt and pain that have derailed us and that we're reluctant to surrender to the Lord. Welcome to The Wayfarer's Inn, Ben." At this Ben sat back and, unlike those who had gone before him, sighed as if some part of a heavy weight had just been lifted off his back.

Turning his attention back to the book once again and tracing his finger down the page, Old Pete called out the name "Fred" as he turned his head toward a table to the right of the fireplace and fixed his gaze upon him and then said, "Fred, I will introduce you next." Without looking up Fred raised his right hand just enough to acknowledge Old Pete. A bespectacled man in his early seventies, Fred had grayish-white, wavy hair and bushy, dark eyebrows. He seemed to all who knew him to be perpetually cranky and to be wearing a permanent scowl. By refusing to meet Old Pete's gaze, Fred was showing a resigned disdain for the whole proceeding. "Fred, it is my understanding that you are the church treasurer." With no response forthcoming Old Pete continued. "In fact, you have been the treasurer for over ten years now. By profession you were an insurance fraud investigator, but you love working with numbers as well. You are known on the governing committee for handing out copies of the budget at every meeting and fastidiously going over it. You especially like looking for overspending on church budget line items." Fred looked back at Old Pete with an intensely suspicious stare while remaining silent. Old Pete met his stare expectantly with a calm, patient look that conveyed to some there, not including Fred, a reassurance that this questioning had a good and higher purpose in mind.

Finally, Fred broke the silence. "You already seem to know a lot about my work at the church," he said in a flat, businesslike tone. "I am not sure if you want me to say anything or not. I gather we're all here, if this whole experience is even real . . ." "Gotta say, Fred, it seems pretty darn real to me," Williard interjected. "I don't know," Fred continued in a snide and derisive tone, "I've had dreams that seemed very real until I woke up. Look, again, I don't know whether this is real or not but on the outside chance it is, well it's pretty clear that we're all in danger of not passing some test of what it means to be a Christian." Fred then stared straight at Old Pete and in an accusatory tone said, "So why don't you save us all a lot of trouble and suspense and just tell us what we need to know to pass it, and then hopefully we can all get out of here." "Show a little respect, Fred, you can be your cranky old self with us. You have leverage, cause as you know all too well, no one else wants your job, but what if this is real . . ." Williard cautioned Fred, his voice trailing off. Old Pete smiled back at Fred in the same calm, patient way, and without answering Fred's question directly said, "The book only gives me some biographical information about each of you, and the roles you've served in, or are currently serving in at the church. It tells me nothing about your innermost feelings or motivations for that service. It is critical to our purpose here that this be discerned by you, as we progress through and past these intros and into a further discussion, which will be led by another."

Fred slumped back and with a weary, resigned tone said, "Look, I pay all the bills for the church, and this carries a heavy responsibility. Some on this committee focus all their energy on the building, mission, or other things, which are all worthy causes, I guess. What they all seem to forget is that in the end a church rises or falls by how well it follows its budget. A key part of my job is keeping the governing committee and the congregation apprised of where we stand with the budget. I also let the congregation know when they're falling behind in their pledges." "You can say that again, talk about negative guilt trips, you get the whole congregation so worked up during the announcements at the start of the service that there's nothing Pastor Jim could say in his sermon to lift their spirits," Ben rebutted in a sarcastic, mocking tone. "That's true, Fred," Debbi said, weighing in, "a lot of the long-term members don't appreciate your diatribes. They come off overbearing and accusatory, especially around the holidays. Frankly you come off a little like Lynn. No offense intended, Lynn," Debbi chirped as she glanced in Lynn's direction. Whereupon Lynn chirped back mockingly, "None taken, Debbi." Unfazed, Debbi continued her pleasant-sounding reprimand of Fred. "Doesn't it say in Scripture that God loves a cheerful giver? Well Fred, our older members don't look very cheerful, do they, by the time you get done. My mother often warned us children that nobody likes a negative Nancy." "I don't think she gets out much," Ben whispered into Lynn's ear. "I have a friend named Nancy and she's real nice," Lynn whispered back, grinning. Not hearing the exchange Debbi continued unfazed, "Besides, I don't think such negative motivation works very well. And as you know most of our long-term members have been giving faithfully for many years." "Yeah, but it's the same amount they gave thirty years ago," Lynn chided audibly. Ignoring Lynn's comment Debbi continued in the same chirpy, at times even syrupy, tone "You do seem awfully cranky a good bit of the time, Fred." "Perhaps a bit more fiber in the diet," Ben followed up, imitating and mocking Debbi's tone.

Sitting up straight and pounding the table with his fist, Fred indicated he had had his fill of the critical feedback. "Enough, you can say whatever you want, but mine is a thankless, time-consuming job, that nobody else wants to do, so fire me or be quiet." Then, leaning forward, and looking up, and after an almost cathartic sigh, Fred added in a more amenable tone, "Besides, my wife says now that I am retired it gets me out of the house and doing something, so at least she seems happy that I am involved at the church." "I bet she is," Ben wisecracked, crossing his legs and clasping his hand behind his head as he sat back in his chair. "What did you mean by that, Ben, why don't you say what you really mean to my face?" "Who me, Fred, what did I say?" Sitting back and folding his arms across his chest defiantly, Fred stared straight ahead with a look of angry frustration.

Old Pete, who had been listening patiently to all that had been said, began to speak again. "Fred, would it be safe to say that maintaining the budget as treasurer has been your primary motivation, if not passion, for serving the church?" "Absolutely," Fred said in an irate tone, still smarting from the feedback he'd just received. "I take great pride in my fiscal service to the church; you might say that I am sharing my gift for working with numbers, and if that makes God happy, that's fine with me too." "Not sure God is that happy with us Fred, I think that might be the whole reason we're here," Ben interjected. "Well, I still don't know why we're here, and until they tell me I am attributing the whole experience to a hard knock on the head," Fred snapped back. "Well Fred, I think at this point it's safe to say that it is no accident that you're sitting here with us at The Wayfarer's Inn, welcome," Old Pete said, concluding the introduction. With a loud har-rumph Fred sat back sullenly in his chair.

Yet again Old Pete turned back to the large leather-bound book and traced his finger down the list on the page. "So, Wes," Old Pete called out as he shifted his gaze to the table where he sat next to Alice, "perhaps it's time we introduced you. You apparently share a similar investment in maintaining the building as Alice." Old Pete had not phrased this as a question, but his momentary pause allowed Wes to respond. "Well, I can't think of any greater overall project to take on than the upkeep of the Lord's house." "Project?" Old Pete repeated in a questioning, curious tone. "That's how I approach every church project or renovation. I was a general contractor before I retired and we moved here," Wes said with obvious pride, puffing out his chest a bit. "Here we go again," Ben sniped. "He's always reminding us of this on the governing committee, I bet he was wonderful to work for." Wes shook his head dismissively at Ben and then continued. "While I admit not everyone appreciates how hard I drove those subcontracted to work under me, I took great pride in the thorough and conscientious way I saw these building projects through to completion." "Now that I am retired, I see myself as bringing this gift to bear in serving the church." "Is that what you call it?" Ben wisecracked under his breath to those sitting at his table. "I now consider myself our church's contractor," Wes said, looking around the room at the committee members anticipating looks of approval. "And," Wes continued, "as our church is now one hundred and fifty years old there will always be more projects to take on if we're to maintain this aging historic building." Then looking again about the room for supportive approval, and with an increasing degree of enthusiasm, Wes added, "Right now we're having restorative work done to the church. Not only is our roof in need of repair, but our fellowship hall needs a new floor, and our aging oil furnace really needs to be replaced. In fact, at our last property committee meeting I laid out the various bids I had I received for a furnace. I also explained in detail how much money we could save with a newer, more efficient oil furnace." Fred's eyes seemed to light up at this as he nodded his head in approval. "Yeah, it took three-quarters of the meeting, and we had to table other pressing issues related to mission and Christian education. A summary from the building committee would have been adequate," Ben called out with his hands cupped around his mouth for emphasis. "I think these are important matters that deserve our full attention," Scott intervened, cutting Ben off abruptly. "Wes is right about the furnace. It's long overdue to be replaced, and its inefficiency no doubt costs us much over the course of the year. It was important that he give us several bids for this at this meeting." As Scott talked on he was unaware that Ben's face had turned red with anger, and with jaw tightly clenched he was glaring angrily at Scott for cutting him off yet again. Old Pete cast Ben an empathetic look and then focused his attention back on Wes. "So, Wes, you've made it clear that you love overseeing the projects in the church. How for you is this tied to an appreciation of the spiritual life of the church?" Old Pete questioned. "You can ask anyone here," Wes responded. "I am in church nearly every Sunday. Most will attest to seeing me regularly standing in the back of the church." "That may be true, Wes, but you never make it through the entire service. I am guessing you disappear to inspect the building," Lynn remarked with a critical edge to her voice. "Maybe, but I try to catch the sermon." "I'll bet if you asked him specifically what he liked about a particular sermon there'd be some serious hemming and hawing," Ben sniped. "How can we expect to grow as a church if we don't keep this building looking nice, let me ask you that?" Wes said defensively, glancing about the room. Old Pete smiled slightly in a bemused way.

Lynn, clearly fed up, in an agitated, shrill tone said, "If I keep saying it maybe it'll sink in. Wes, has it ever occurred to you, that you might end up with a beautiful building and no congregation? A lot of beautiful, well-maintained churches these days are having to close their doors these days due to declining attendance." Wes did not respond, but paused, his face taking on a look of consternation as if for the first time he considered this a possibility. After a few moments Old Pete weighed in, "Well, Wes, you've been clear about where your passion lies regarding the church, and how it motivates your service to the church. Suffice it to say you ended up at the right place. Welcome to The Wayfarer's Inn."

Returning to the list in the large, leather-bound book once more, Old Pete traced his finger down the list. Then looking out on the assembly, he announced, "I would like to introduce Evelyn next." Old Pete directed his gaze toward an elderly woman seated at the table nearest the Christmas tree in the far-right back corner of the room. Old Pete's gaze had settled on a white-haired woman in her early eighties, her advanced age made less apparent by her dignified carriage and the esteem with which she was held by many church members. Her beautifully coiffed white hair and refined dress lent an air of elegance and sophistication to her overall appearance. "Evelyn, I understand both you and your husband grew up in the church, and that you were married there. It is also my understanding that you had been married for over fifty years until your husband passed away a few years ago." An approving murmur arose from those seated at the tables around the room. Old Pete then continued. "You have a particular passion for preserving the traditional roles of the deacons and elders as well as the acolytes, congregation, and pastor. Your passion for preserving past traditions also extends to the liturgy as well." "That is true," Evelyn replied. "There is a growing lack of reverence toward worship in our church. Crying babies are often not removed, when they disrupt the service; deacons and elders no longer fulfill their traditional functions on Sunday mornings and on special occasions in the life of our church. Also, Pastor Jim is increasingly replacing our traditional liturgical responses with contemporary liturgies that he tells us are more relevant for our time. A lot of people have come to me and complained about this, particularly our older members."

"I see," Old Pete responded. "What about all this bothers you so much?" "Well, let's start with the elders and deacons. There should be twelve in church every Sunday morning. We're lucky if half that number show up." "It might help if the nominating committee actually picked people for the governing committee who were invested in the spiritual life of the church," Ben whispered, leaning toward Lynn. "And Pastor Jim should see to it that they all sit up front together in the same pew as they did when I was a girl," Evelyn continued. Lifting and cocking his head up and to one side, while squinting one eye, Ben feigned the look of one trying to count just how far back that would be. "In fact, I blame a lot of this on the pastor; if our committee members were better instructed and organized in their duties, we wouldn't have all these problems." "I do go over the duties of elders and deacons when they first come on the committee, Evelyn, but I can't force them to do some of these things. Nor do I share your belief that all of their traditional duties are still relevant to our times," Pastor Jim interrupted with a weary defensiveness as he slumped back in his chair. "Well, Pastor Bill was able to preserve these traditions over the many years he was our pastor, at least more so than you." Pastor Jim slumped further back in his chair, looked down and shook his head. Jumping to his defense, Lynn shot back, "That's only because for most of the thirty years he was our pastor your generation was still around, and still relished being in these roles." Evelyn acted as if she had not heard her remarks. "I don't think she heard you, Lynn," Ben whispered to Lynn. "Either that or she doesn't want to hear us. We've said these things to her before." Evelyn's diatribe continued.

"I have also been noticing a growing lack of reverence toward worship in our church on the part of many in our congregation. Worship should be a solemn, reverent affair. Why, only a few Sundays back the acolyte, one of our confirmands, wore the most awful green sneakers up into the chancel, and they appeared to be twinkling. In my day that would have been un-thinkable. Also, an increasing number of people dress casually when they come to church—some even wear jeans. One new member, a huge, burly fellow with long hair, wears a sleeveless jean jacket and has tattoos covering both arms. He looks like a member of one of those biker gangs," Evelyn huffed. "I don't know, Evelyn, Fred might be able to use him during the annual stewardship drive. Imagine him showing up at the doors of those folk who always turn in their pledge cards late?" Ben wisecracked with a mischievous grin. Ignoring or not hearing, Evelyn then offered what for her was a prime example of proper church behavior. "Thankfully, there are some young people that set a better example. We now have two new visitors, two clean-cut young men who sit near the front. Well-dressed, they conduct themselves in a refined, polite, and respectful way." At this Ben leaned toward Lynn and whispered in her ear, "I don't think she's aware that they're gay, they haven't exactly kept this a secret. Should we enlighten her?" "No," Lynn cautioned, "not sure she could handle it. Some of the other older ladies have been commenting on the wonderful example they've been setting as well. Without knowing it, they're reinforcing a stereotype of gay men." "Once they find out they're gay, we're going to hear a lot of clucking in the hen house." "Ben," Lynn chided, "that's not nice or fair and you might be surprised, deafness aside, at how open minded some of these older church lady types can be. My grandmother was one of them. Once when I was a child, and my father criticized women for working outside the home, my grandmother scolded him, 'and why not!' She then reminded him that both husband and wife often must work these days just to make ends meet. In any case these older ladies will find out soon enough," Lynn whispered back as she tilted her head toward Ben.

"I won't say any more about the liturgy," Evelyn then said as she continued her harangue. "I think Pastor Jim knows how I feel. Although I will say this, Pastor Jim recently referred to God in the female gender in the Lord's Prayer. Can you imagine that, everyone knows God's male. It's all through the Bible." "Actually, Evelyn, the Old Testament word often used for God's Spirit, *ruach*, is a Hebrew word that denotes a feminine nature," Pastor Jim instructed. "Also, I've tried explaining to you and others that these are just anthropomorphisms for God, who transcends all such personas." "Yeah, but I don't think he ever explained to her what anthropomorphisms means, or personas for that matter," Ben whispered to Lynn. "Language is important, Evelyn," Pastor Jim followed up in a more conciliatory tone, "especially for our older members who cherish the older, rote liturgies. I realize it offers some comfort to these members, in a worship context, and that at least some things don't change too quickly. I try to walk a fine line between the needs of the new, younger members, if we want to hold onto them, who want liturgies that speak to them, and some older members who are resistant to any changes to the liturgy. Also, as you all know I would like to start a separate, earlier contemporary service for those who prefer that. This, however, would require moving our regular service to a slightly later time to accommodate parents with children. There has been, suffice to say, much resistance to such a change." "Well all I know," Evelyn said with a huff, "is that in my day, and when I was a child, the church didn't have to cater to such folk. People came to worship God for all the right reasons. Worship wasn't seen as entertainment back then. They didn't get bored so easily." "Oh, I am pretty sure they were bored stiff, especially when the preacher's sermons went on too long on those hot, humid summer Sundays. They just didn't know what to call it and thought it unacceptable to challenge it, no frame of reference," Ben whispered to Lynn. "I know for a fact the kids were bored stiff," Lynn whispered back, adding, "when my grandfather was a boy, he and some of the other boys in the balcony would tie thread to the feet of horse flies they'd caught and then release them over the congregation. This weighted them down just enough so that as they flew over the worshipers the thread would flit across the heads of the congregation, causing them to look up in annoyance. My grandfather told me the pastor, a starch-collared old time preacher, with most of his distracted congregation staring heavenward, actually stopped his sermon to scold the boys." Ben smiled and whispered back, "Well, even if that kind of service was all they knew, I guess kids will be kids no matter the era." Old Pete as usual had been listening patiently to Evelyn while being aware of background banter. He had allowed some clearing of the air so that a more fruitful later discussion might happen. Sensing things were winding down he spoke again. "So, Evelyn, if I understand you correctly, your passion for serving the governing committee and church is to preserve a traditional style of church leadership and worship, is that correct?" "Yes indeed," Evelyn responded plaintively. "I think what bothers me and others most is the lack of reverence for worship and our religious traditions." "So," Old Pete remarked, "by religion do you mean the faith?" "Same difference," Evelyn snapped back. "Perhaps if you were as old as I am you would understand better how important maintaining a religious tradition is." Smiling in a bemused way, Old Pete answered, "You might be surprised if I told you just how old I am. In the very earliest days of the church there wasn't a fixed liturgy, or black and white church doctrines, and those that worshiped were a diverse crowd. We met in the homes, worshiped, sang, read what we had concerning Jesus' teachings and ministry, and witnessed to the hope and joy that we found in 'The Way.'" "The Way?" several governing committee members asked in a puzzled tone. "The Way was what we called the early Christian church. It was more of a movement then. Being a Christian at that time was more of a verb than a noun, a way of life both for the individual and faith community. It was more about passionately living your faith, despite the threat of persecution and even death." "He can't be," a majority of members murmured to each other. "I thought so right from the start just from the name that that's who he was," Clark whispered to Scott. "He looks good for his age," Williard could be heard whispering. "The possibility probably occurred to all of us, but initially I, for one, just kept hoping I'd wake up at any moment," Scott whispered audibly. "Well," Old Pete said, smiling, having allowed for a few moments of silence, "we're nearly at the end of the introductions." Then turning back toward Evelyn, he said, "Evelyn, suffice it to say your journey too has brought you to the right place. Welcome to The Wayfarer's Inn."

After a brief pause Old Pete continued, "We now have only Pastor Jim to turn to." "I thought you might be saving the worst for last," Pastor Jim joked. "There is no worst, Jim," Old Pete responded, "but if you're ready let's begin. I will be sharing a bit more of your history if that's okay?" Old Pete said, then pausing. Jim sat upright in his chair, giving Old Pete his full attention while appearing concerned. "I have tried to keep much of my personal life private, particularly related to my faith journey, as this might not be helpful to the committee or my congregation. Is this necessary?" Jim added. "It could be very helpful to this group, Jim," Old Pete responded. "Your church leadership and to some extent your faith community is experiencing much tension and conflict. At this point and given where you find yourself, opening up and being honest and genuine about your faith journey is also important for you to arrive at deeper insights and spiritual growth." "Maybe so, but couldn't it also further undermine any standing I have with the committee, at a time where my leadership is most needed?" Jim responded. "Jim," Old Pete replied patiently but persistently, "the question of what motivates you and makes you passionate as a Christian leader might well determine whether you lead your flock away from or toward a vital faith relationship with Jesus Christ, both as individuals and a faith community. Also, the faith struggles you share with us might well offer up valuable insights both for yourself and your committee members." "Well, I guess, given where things are at," Jim said as he looked around the room at the committee members, "all of us might benefit from a little collective soul searching at this point. A little Divine intervention might not hurt either, if that's what going on here. Besides, what do we have left to lose," Jim added with a hint of self-deprecation. "I don't know, though, if this group is ready to be that vulnerable when it's hard for them to constructively share their differences. If there is anything I've learned as a pastor, particularly in this church, it's been to pick my battles carefully, and let a lot of other, lesser conflicts go by." "Don't you mean sweep them under the carpet, Pastor?" Ben interjected in the more respectful tone he reserved for Pastor Jim. "I worry that by sweeping so much under the carpet we have allowed much anger to simmer among the congregation that only gets expressed passive aggressively behind people's backs. Nothing ever gets resolved this way. Besides, some of these so-called lesser issues can get blown way out of proportion that way. Many of our folk confuse what they call 'the honest truth' with subjective opinion. Denying such issues exist has made it impossible to move past them so that we can share our vulnerabilities in the light of God's saving grace. It might only be then, collectively enabled by that grace, that we would be able to see and discuss the deeper spiritual issues we desperately need to acknowledge."

A sudden, incongruous thought then occurred to Jim, and he voiced it to Ben. "You had already shared something of your personal faith journey, and vulnerabilities. If this is part of what we're about here, I should have been the first to set this example even at the risk of undermining my pastoral status further. It is shaping up to be a critical exercise if we are to have any chance of resuming our spiritual journeys. Perhaps God's grace needs to transform us more deeply and holistically than any of us had imagined." "While I think what you just said is probably true," Ben responded, "I am not sure I agree that you needed to be the one to set an example here. I believe it reminds us in 1 Peter 1:13–20 that 'we are all ministers in the Lord.' You might be called to some special functions as pastor, but you should never be seen as a hired spiritual gun, the one most expected to set a Christian example for the rest of us, and consequently put up on a pedestal. Isn't that what the priesthood of all believers is meant to challenge?" "Of course, you're right Ben, and your example, hopefully together with what I am about to share, will encourage others, given our level of conflict and this setting, to risk being vulnerable.

"As Old Pete is still in the process of introducing me, let me now share something more personal about my faith journey." Old Pete nodded his head encouragingly. "Again, I think it important that Jim share something of his own faith journey. Like Ben, he has given considerable reflection to this journey. A discussion will follow these introductions where hopefully all of you will feel more enabled to share openly and honestly about your respective faith journeys. What Ben shared, and Pastor Jim is about to share, will help us transition to the discussion that follows. My purpose here, apart from welcoming you and facilitating these introductions, is to prime the pump, so to speak, to allow some discord to surface and clear the air for the discussion to follow. It is also to help you establish a baseline, which affords perspective as you grow spiritually. It might also help you see as well how far you've come when tempted to re-embrace, or totally abandon, old religious investments that no longer represent where you really are on your faith journey, confusing and scary as that might be.

"So, Jim, you grew up in a very religious home, where prayer, Scripture readings, and Christian values were practiced and modeled in everyday life. Your parents were good about not indoctrinating you into a narrow set of black and white faith beliefs but emphasized what they saw as the heart of the faith, God's love, saving grace, and forgiveness in Jesus Christ. Even when disciplining your sister and you they focused on actions and issues and never condemned your sister or you as individuals. They made sure you knew you were unconditionally loved. So far, so good?" Old Pete inquired. "So far, so good," Jim responded, "but here's a little more bio, and in case anybody was wondering how old I am. I was born in 1979 and grew up in a small town in Illinois, in a wonderful nuclear family. There was a lot of love and security, and for this I will always be grateful, and while my parents weren't perfect, they strove to live their faith in humble, nonjudgmental ways. They modeled this for my sister and me, and I have tried to make this an integral part of my ministry style.

Through high school I began to question my childhood faith beliefs, even as I continued to attend church and was active in the youth group. After starting college in 1998 these questions continued to grow in direct proportion to the faith doubts that sparked them. This was, I am sure, in no small part influenced by an increasingly secular culture pervaded by the modern scientific world view. My questions grew increasingly sophisticated, nuanced, and called forth equally sophisticated theological and philosophical answers. While in college I began reading the works of Christian apologists, you know, writers and debaters who defend scriptural integrity and the faith with rigorous logical arguments. Strangely, despite my increasing questions and doubts, I still felt that a career in ministry best fit my aptitudes and quest for ultimate meaning and purpose in my life.

"Later in seminary I took classes in theology, philosophy, and Old and New Testament biblical studies, among other required subjects. The biblical studies classes were for the most part taught from a purely objective, scholarly perspective. At the time I assumed that all such scholars were also great people of faith. I have since learned at least some were not. One, often utilized as an expert in what are advertised in the media as 'Christian documentaries,' has since self-identified as an agnostic. What I fear is the case with some of these scholars is that they are more into deconstructing Scripture from a purely empirical, scholarly perspective than exploring it from a divinely inspired, scripturally coherent perspective as it relates to a passage, the New Testament, or the entire canon. They also seemed to be heavily influenced by a still culturally pervasive modern scientific world-view that rules out any supernatural explanations, even for those Gospel texts that affirm core Christian beliefs. While I am well aware of this now, back in seminary this strongly reinforced my need to find rational justifications for my faith. For a while I turned back to the Christian apologists as a counter influence.

"Their arguments no longer sufficing to quell my deepening faith doubts, I somewhat reluctantly at first embraced the most liberal brand of biblical scholarship I had encountered at the seminary. After all, I reasoned, it is almost invulnerable to faith doubt, as it views Scripture entirely through the lens of metaphorical interpretation that does not allow for any supernatural explanations. This in essence reduces Jesus to the status of a great ethical teacher. I wasn't deist, but at the time removing a God who personally interacts with us appealed to a part of me. I even had a copy of Thomas Jefferson's, who was a deist, *The Life and Morals of Jesus of Nazareth* revision of the New Testament. It consisted primarily of Jesus' teachings and excluded any supernatural explanation.

"I reassured myself that I could offer my parishioners spiritual meaning and insight symbolically and metaphorically through my preaching and teaching, without them needing to know that for me, any literal, historical, and traditional New Testament foundational pillars for these interpretations were crumbling or gone. I bought their arguments without fully realizing that, rather than hopefully offering some substitute foundation to shore up my faith, they were really deconstructing that faith further.

"My more devout Christian friends encouraged me to read the works of moderate biblical and theological scholars, such N. T. Wright and Luke Timothy Johnson, who exposed biased empirical interpretations, presuppositions, and the self-righteousness implicit in this brand of so-called liberal scholarship, albeit replacing these with their own interpretations. They also tried to make me aware that the unwitting or hidden agenda of such scholarship was to make the Gospels more compatible with the modern scientific worldview, rather than confronting the enthronement and absolutizing of reason and with it the extinguishing of all religious understandings and spirituality. My addiction to finding rational arguments for the faith to counter my faith doubts only grew after seminary and into my ministry years. Evidence of this addiction pervaded my teaching and preaching ministry. Worse yet, I felt little motivation to perform the pastoral care aspects of ministry, visitation, and counseling, where people were often in desperate need of a comforting word of faith or a prayer. I derived more of a sense of pride and purpose from performing my duties as a trained professional than from any deeper sense of a spiritual call. My sermons were written and preached more to convince myself intellectually that I still had some mandate to continue as a pastor." "Well, that explains why most of your sermons went over our heads," Wes said, breaking into Pastor Jim's lengthening monologue.

Unfazed, Jim continued, "Deep down I think I knew all along that I was deluding myself and misleading my congregation at a critical time and juncture in the life of their church. I had found over time that no matter how sophisticated the scholarly or intellectual the argument, in the end they didn't resolve my doubts for long, much less result in a passionately lived faith life. At best they only succeeded in reinforcing my denial and suppression of what I, deep down, knew to be true, that it was all a façade, an idolatrous substitution and elevation of reason over a lived personal relationship with Jesus Christ. Deep down I've always suspected that what Paul says in 1 Corinthians 15 is true, that if you don't have faith in the resurrection, the tower of cards you've built out of any substitutionary intellectual arguments, church institutional trappings, or other faith substitutes will sooner or later collapse. I learned from some of my theological readings, namely Kierkegaard and Henri Nouwen, in seminary that faith is not the same as merely claiming to be an adherent of some religious traditions or set of beliefs. We are given the free will to accept or reject God's love, else it would not measure up to any Divine-human relational, scriptural understanding of agape love. True faith, I am beginning to see, comes down to the individual's radical decision to accept God's love in Jesus Christ and to passionately live out that faith despite one's faith doubts. Faith then no longer being confused with certainty of belief, but relying more on trusting God and living out our faith despite an inevitable lack of rational and empirical proofs.

"And yet, as much as my evolving theology appeals to me, I haven't been able to bring myself to make that radical faith decision I just referred to. Consequently, it was reduced to just another example of all my other intellectual justifications for faith. Sometimes I wonder if my problem is that I overthink all these things." "No, not you," Ben teased, evoking a ripple of laughter. "Some time, Pastor, let me share memories of my grandmother, who only graduated from the eighth grade and was beloved as a gentle, kind, nurturing soul. She was also a deeply devout Christian who lived and breathed her faith. She was able to grasp the heart of the gospel without being learned in the faith," Ben added. "I get your point, Ben," Pastor Jim replied. "Regardless, I now find myself in a spiritual limbo where intellectual rationales for my faith no longer suffice, and where the questions my faith doubts raise, or vice versa, keep me from making a decision to prayerfully strive to passionately live out my faith.

"Well, there you have it, I've honestly shared more than I thought I would, and frankly it feels good. Is there anything else you would like to know?" Jim said, glancing first at Old Pete and then around the room. "No, I think that about says it," Wes quipped sarcastically, adding, "thanks for sharing, Fred's chin is on his chest. He looks like he just saw something crawl into his belly button, and the rest of us looked like a group of pigeons feeding with our heads bobbing up and down." "Lynn and I didn't," Ben snapped back. Old Pete, ignoring Wes's oblivious sniping, remained focused on Jim. "Well Pastor Jim, it took great courage to share as you did and freed me from having to do more of an intro for you. You honestly shared that what motivated you to serve your church as a pastor has been an intellectual, rationally driven need to justify your faith. Your faith struggles clearly appear to have left you weary and in despair. The retreat you planned no doubt would have added to that weariness and despair. Jim, welcome to The Wayfarer's Inn. You are more aware than most that it is no accident that your journey brought you here, and this may help you, but it also appears to have waylaid you here."

After concluding Pastor Jim's introduction and welcome, Old Pete came round the far end of the bar and walked to the middle of the front of the bar and leaned back on the bar stool there. Momentarily silent, he smiled in a warm, accepting, and compassionate way as he surveyed the faces at each of the tables. After a few more moments of silence, he addressed the expectant faces looking up at him. "Well, that about wraps up your introductions and again, welcome to The Wayfarer's Inn. Thank you for allowing me to make these introductions, especially given how strange your experience here must seem to you." As Old Pete made these concluding remarks Ben appeared lost in thought, his brow furrowed, and with a puzzled look on his face he suddenly spoke out, interrupting Old Pete's concluding remarks. "Old Pete, near the end of each of our introductions you asked most of us what our passion was for serving the church. Can you clarify what exactly you meant by that? I used to feel passionate about being a Christian, but I am not sure I do anymore. Perhaps it wasn't even the kind of passion you're referring to."

Old Pete smiled back knowingly at Ben. "I had been hoping one of you would ask that question," he answered. "Having said that, though, and consistent with our approach here, I would rather one of you attempted to answer this. I realize, however, that most of you may not have given this question much thought." Turning to Pastor Jim, Old Pete then suggested, "Jim, you have wrestled arduously with many questions of faith, perhaps you might help us reflect on this question." Pastor Jim looked up at Old Pete and met his gaze. "I may end up disappointing all of you, but I will try to share something of my past reflections, and where I am at now, as it relates to this question. My answer more specifically has to do with it means to have passionate faith in the context of a relationship with Jesus Christ. I can only answer this for myself; you all will have to decide whether you resonate with any of what I am about to say. Also, if I am honest, these are largely abstract, intellectual understandings that I have yet to apply to my life. Be patient with me, as I have a tendency to go off on tangents." "No, say it's not true," a chorus of voices answered back. "At least I am aware of it, and in the end these tangents mostly relate back to the question at hand," Pastor Jim added in whiny, defensive tone. "Before I say any more, though, let me share with you the one thing that Christian passion should never be confused with, and that is with the histrionic religious emotionalism of the spiritually immature. If I had to compare true Christian passion to anything it would be like the strong, flowing waters of an underground spring that surfaces whenever we prayerfully awaken to our parched, thirsting soul within, that only its water can quench.

"As long as I can remember I have experienced a drive, you could call it a passion, to fully seek and embrace the Christian truth, at the heart of which is the person, work, and ministry of Jesus Christ. I felt this drive even amid the most overwhelming doubt. It could also be described as an undying hope. A deep, questing hope that somehow reassured me that, once fulfilled, it alone could answer my deepest needs for ultimate meaning and purpose in life. Also wrapped up in this drive was a deep desire to be loved and accepted just as I was with all my faults and insecurities. I am not saying that I always felt this passion, but to use a follow-up analogy, like a prayer-cup of refreshing spring water I always knew it was there, ready to refresh my thirsting soul. As my questions and doubts grew in college and seminary, I increasingly tried to counter them with the biblical, theological, and philosophical answers. But these arguments never seemed to keep my doubts at bay for long, in fact most just raised troubling new questions. Without being fully aware of it I had become increasingly reliant on such arguments to shore up my faith. Unconsciously I was channeling that desire, that undying hope, that passion into pursuing and attempting to establish a purely rational basis by which to sustain my faith. I have recently come to accept that this misdirected passion will never accomplish this goal, nor was it fulfilling the deeper needs already mentioned. Instead of sustaining my passion to come to know the Lord, a deep despair was gradually setting in. It occurred to me that if my soul is eternal, then trying to satiate it with worldly externals, rational justification for faith included, it's no wonder that this has resulted in failure and despair. Maybe, though, a relationship with the soul's ultimate source and destination through Jesus Christ could fulfill such an inner and subjective passion. In the meantime, other troubling questions more grounded in my everyday reality came to plague me. How could I keep pretending that I felt a genuine call to ministry. I felt like a fraud.

"This all has led to some insights related to the nature of Christian passion. What I had to confront, in myself, and accept, is that I had totally externalized my faith. I had become entirely dependent on scholarly arguments to salvage and validate my faith. In short, I was trying to become a Christian from the outside in. I also began to see record numbers of traditional Christians, nominal Christians, and non-institutional Christians doing the same thing. In different ways they were transferring and misdirecting this created, innate, and fundamental drive or passion into and onto externals such as black and white belief systems, church traditions, politicizations, institutional trappings, or an eclectic spiritualism stripped bare of any healthy informative and coherent context. By externalizing their faith, like me, they were also objectifying it, treating it as something they could control, and which could not as easily be threatened by rampant secularism and scientism, the hijacked scientific method that presupposes a materialistic universe as the only thing that can be proven to be real and true. I am now reconsidering that the most essential core Christian truths, the incarnation, resurrection, our atonement and salvation, the gift of the Holy Spirit and our guidance by it toward spiritual maturity and growth, can be neither proven nor disproven scientifically. These are truths we must accept on faith that lies outside the domain of scientific materialism, much as do the virtues of justice, equality, and freedom, and the democratic system of government that enshrines them. Yet strangely these equally non-materialistic, often absolutized ideals and framework seldom get questioned.

"I also have concluded that neither external intellectual abstractions like mine nor any other externalized religious beliefs by themselves will, in the long run, preserve the faith community we call the church. There was one theologian I studied in seminary who planted some seeds for reflection in me that are just beginning to germinate. He wrote something about the nature of truth. That for truth to be truth for us it has to be wholly subjective and personal. I understood this to mean that only then can we experience that truth holistically and transformatively for our life. In short, from the inside out. For the Christian this can only happen within a lived out relationship with Jesus Christ. Or to state it another way the Christian faith was never meant to be a spectator sport where a superficial adherence of some religious kind could ever replace a personal relationship with Christ. As Christians we can argue all we want about the lesser evolving traditions of the faith, but I hope in time we come to agree on this."

"Pastor, you briefly shared your experience and understanding of Christian passion, but then you mostly talked about how that passion can be easily misdirected and channeled into religious externals," Ben said, interrupting Jim. "To get us back on track and ground what you're saying in Scripture, could you say a little about what the Bible has to say about this passion?" "Really, Ben," Wes sniped in a disgusted tone, "you had to ask him another question just when he was beginning to wind down." Desensitized to such remarks from Wes, and secretly flattered by Ben's question, which appealed to a part of him that had once aspired to be a professor, Jim plowed ahead.

"First, we must distinguish between Christ's passion on the cross and what Scripture alludes to as the passion of the heart in, among other places, Ephesians 4:31. Paul alludes to the latter as well in Romans 2:28 and 29 where he draws a contrast between those who worship the letter of the law externally and those who worship God in spirit from the heart. Paul is building on an Old Testament text from Deuteronomy 10:16, 'Therefore circumcise the foreskin of the heart,' which implies the need for spiritual renewal on the part of the people of Israel, circumcision originally having to do with Abraham's covenant with God requiring this rite of all males and future generations. The heart in Scripture is a symbol of life, unity of self, and spiritual passion." "Please Pastor," Williard interrupted in a pleading tone, "could you also give us a concrete, everyday illustration of what is meant in these passages?" Jim's face turned red and with a sheepish look on his face he said, "I hear you; I'll try.

"I have often found in prolonged conversations with friends that once we're done talking about superficialities, such as the weather or sports, they would turn the discussion toward some topic they felt strongly or passionately about. In my discussions with friends who are also people of faith, what often became apparent was their need to share something of the hope, love, and joy afforded to them by their faith in Christ. What also became clear was their desire, uplifted by God's saving grace, to model their lives after the example Christ modeled for us where He was driven passionately to fulfill His mission on earth. This was particularly evident in the compassion and grace Jesus showed toward the sick, marginalized, poor, and oppressed. So, it has become clear to me that the truly passionate Christian is never content to keep God's love and grace for themselves or those most like them, but to share it in ever widening, non-discriminating relational circles. I might add in ways observant of context and where a person is at, or not, faith wise." "I have one more question for you Pastor, regarding Christian passion." Hearing this a collective groan, minus Jim, arose from the head table. "One thing troubles me now as I think more about the nature of Christian passion. How can us mere humans, even with empowerment of God's grace, possibly sustain that passion given all of life's challenges?" That's a fair and important question, Ben," Jim answered. "That's where still relevant and vital religious traditions and practices, as long as they don't supersede or worse, suffocate, the living faith they're meant to nurture and harbor, can be instrumental. We are, after all, innately creatures of habit and ritual, and those religious traditions and practices that still hold relevance and have the vitality to re-center us spiritually, or at least keep us facing toward God amid a faith crisis or wilderness experience, can be of great value. To sum up, there are really three aspects to a Christian's passion of the heart: the passion that seeks a relationship with Christ, the passion to live that relationship, and the passion to share it. Although they are three aspects of one continuous, often overlapping, and even co-occurring passion that no abstraction can do justice to." "One last question just occurred to me," Ben then asked in an unrushed tone, unaffected by the complaining utterances around the room. Wes let out a guttural moan and then looked over toward Old Pete and whined, "How long are you going to let this go on?" Old Pete smiled in an understanding way but refused to intervene. "Drink some more of the beer, Wes. That's what it's for," Ben chided without turning his head toward Wes.

"Pastor, given all the insights and understandings you've shared with us, how is it possible that you, of all people, are still plagued by doubts?" "I should have seen that question coming, Ben. Here's my honest answer. God gifted us with free will. Part of exercising that free will is counting the cost of a passionate, lived out relationship with Christ. Despite all my studies, reflections, and insights or perhaps because of them, there is one thing that I have had trouble surrendering to God, and as I am sure you now know, that is my need to rationally justify my faith. The very insights that you may find helpful for me are the by-product of a deeply ingrained habit, one where I subverted and misdirected the desire God placed within me to come to know His/Her love in Jesus Christ, into an obsession with trying to justify my faith through theological and philosophical rationalizations." Jim let out a long, weary sigh and said, "Well, I've done it again, gone off on tangents and talked way too much." "Don't sell yourself short," Ben wisecracked. "You probably talked over our heads as well. I am only joking, I am partially at fault here," Ben quickly added.

"While I can't say they took in everything you just said, they're still awake. Neither do they look quite as bored and annoyed as they often have in the past, that is, except for Fred who looks even more pissed off than usual. I think some of what you just shared might have resonated with most of them. I gotta say Pastor, I understand much better now how much you've struggled and suffered on your faith journey." Jim remained quiet.

A silence followed. Old Pete then broke the silence. "Jim, what you have shared has provided some excellent fodder for the discussion to follow." "There's another one," Wes whined. "I feel like I am back in school." "That's okay," Ben wisecracked, "if the headaches come back, we'll know why." Old Pete had clearly indicated his approval of the extended discussion Ben's questions had elicited. He had listened patiently to the answers Pastor Jim had given to Ben's questions. He now spoke again. Old Pete then instructed them to move some tables aside and put their chairs in a circle, leaving one chair empty at the head of the circle in front of the bar counter. Old Pete waited patiently until they had done this and were all seated in the newly formed circle. He then spoke again. "Once more let me say it has been my honor and privilege to welcome and introduce you here at The Wayfarer's Inn. It has also been my purpose here to help prepare you for the discussion to come. I will not be leading this discussion. The Innkeeper has taken this on Himself/Herself." As Old Pete uttered these words a muffled sound could be heard in the room behind the staff door. "I believe that's the Innkeeper now. I must now take my leave of you. I hope and pray you find your stay here inspiring and enlightening and that you will open your hearts and minds to each other and the Innkeeper." With that, Old Pete waved goodbye and headed toward the Staff door. Though somewhat subdued, the committee voiced their gratitude and waved back as he walked toward the Staff door and exited. Their anxious anticipation of who and what was to follow, along with the mystery that enveloped their whole experience at the Inn, muted what might otherwise have been a heartier farewell. As they waited, brief conversations broke out as to what that experience was about, what was expected of them, and how it would all end. Most admitted to each other that this was clearly meant to be a shared experience. Fred even admitted to having pinched himself a couple times to try to wake himself up. It hadn't worked.

Adam's Question

SOON THEY HEARD THE creaking hinges of the large, wooden Staff door as it began to open. They turned their heads in the direction of the door and waited with bated breath to see who was about to walk through. Most, having heard him referred to as the Innkeeper, were expecting a wizened older man to appear. They were startled then to see a young man, who appeared to be in his early thirties, come through the door. He had long black hair, an olive complexion, and was above average height. But what caught everyone's attention almost immediately were his eyes. Deep brown in color, they would have the uncanny effect on each committee member of seeming to look directly into their souls, while simultaneously conveying a depthless compassion. As he looked at each committee member in turn, he conveyed the intuitive sense that he knew them better than they knew themselves. As they had been instructed, a chair had been left empty at the head of the circle, and he made his way over to it and sat down. He then smiled and said, "I know you were expecting my Father, but He chose me to represent Him. Some have called me Adam the Second, but you may just call me Adam." "Welcome, Adam," the circle of voices said in unison. All, given the name, were aware of who this had to be. Accepting that God's hand was most likely at work here, and not wanting to disrupt the agenda planned for them, they kept this to themselves.

Adam nodded his head and smiled warmly in response and spoke again. "As you probably know by now it is no accident that you are here. The Innkeeper wants you to know that He is doing all He can to prepare you for the rest of your journey. However, while guided, you will not be coerced to do or commit to anything against your will. This would not be consistent with the nature of His love for each one of you. I will be leading a discussion where you will all hopefully arrive at deeper understandings, individually and collectively, of what it means to be a Christian. But as you will not be coerced to arrive at these understandings you will have to do much of the work yourself. This will require an open-mindedness to serious reflection that will involve heart, mind, and spirit. I will be asking you an overarching question as well as subsequent questions that may make you reconsider the underlying motivations for your church involvements, investments, and service. Hopefully Old Pete's introductions and welcome gave you the opportunity to reflect on why you are here, as well as to air some of the tensions that have so divided you as a committee and church members. From here on it will be important for each of you to focus more on yourselves, and less on others. You may point out a contradiction in someone's thinking, but speak directly to them, and do so with the goal of helping them to clarify their thinking and your own, and not to put them down or force your views on them. You should see yourselves as spiritual midwives who, rather than arguing with each other, should seek to help one another arrive at a deeper, more profound understanding of what it means to be a Christian. I know this will not be easy as the world you know has habituated you toward polarizing arguments. Eat heartily of the bread, and drink deeply of the beer, and with my assistance you should find this task easier.

"Before we begin the dialogue, let me make a few more comments. I am about to put the afore referenced question to each of you again. Your answers may differ considerably, especially your initial answers. Without too much forethought, and as honestly as you can, give me your answer to the question. It is okay to answer this question right off the top of your head. It is important for you to clearly discern what you still regard to some extent as the answer to the question. Please be reassured again that no one here will be forced to answer; that must be your decision as well. Know too there is nothing wrong with wanting to use your gifts in service to the church, but hopefully a deeper, underlying understanding and spiritual awareness will frame and inform the Spirit in which you employ these gifts. Finally, much critical thinking and discussion may be prompted both by the questions asked by me and by those you raise with each other. Please don't mistake, though, this phase of your stay here as an end to your spiritual growth and development. The discussion that follows may further confuse you at times. It is likely you will not be able to succinctly articulate or reach an agreed upon understanding of what it means to be a Christian. Arriving at deeper understandings, individually or collectively, is only an important first step, and must be further informed by lived out experiences of faith and the profound insights they afford. Finally, letting go of substitute investments for a holistic personal relationship with Christ is a process. Hopefully a prayer-driven one. These investments are often most fiercely defended when they've been exposed for what they are, but this can also be the darkness before the dawn."

Adam paused and looked searchingly at the expectant faces around the circle. They intuitively sensed that he knew the content of their hearts. His discerning gaze invoked in them a sense of trust. While appearing as human as all there, he projected an ineffable spiritual authority and otherworldly aura. Most knew, although perhaps not at first, that more was about to be shared than the initial, superficial understandings and conflicts that had so characterized the discussion when Old Pete was present. Adam then turned to Pastor Jim and asked, "Jim would you mind starting us off with prayer?" "No, of course not," he responded appearing a bit sheepish and wondering, given all that he had shared, whether his committee members still had any respect for him or looked to him anymore as their pastor. "Remember to keep it short, Pastor, as we apparently have another intense discussion ahead," Alice sniped out of habit, prompting Adam to give her a calm but firm, penetrating look that immediately caused her to mutter an apology and lower her head.

With the prayer over Adam spoke again: "In the discussion that follows you will no doubt be sidetracked, and contentiousness may yet arise, but try not to lose sight of the question at hand. The question I now ask each of you is, What does it mean to you personally to say that you are a Christian?" Debbi waved her hand in the air. "I think I know," she said, again looking like an overly enthusiastic schoolgirl who is sure she has the right answer. With a nod of his head Adam prompted her to continue. "I associate being a Christian with long-term membership in a church community. This not only shows your commitment to the church but to the faith." "I see," Ben remarked in as even keel a tone of voice as he could. "So, depending on what you consider long term, some members of this committee might not meet that definition. Come to think of it I don't think even Jesus' disciples and His followers during His ministry on earth by this definition could be considered Christians. During Jesus' ministry on earth there was no church as we know it, and Jesus spent much of His time teaching and preaching in the fields and hills surrounding Galilee," Ben added. "I guess I didn't think my answer through so well," Debbi responded after a moment's pause, as she glanced sheepishly at the others around the circle. She then perked up a bit as she thought of a better way to phrase her answer that might resolve objections to it. "What I meant to say was that when someone, these days, has been a long-term member of a church, that would certainly seem to offer concrete proof of their Christian faith commitment." "Would you concede," Pastor Jim pushed back gently, "that many churches, ours included, have long-standing members who offer, by their words and actions, much counter evidence to a faith life centered around a relationship with Jesus Christ?" "I guess I didn't think that answer out too well either," Debbi replied, as her face reddened. "Debbi," Adam reassured, "the point of these questions is not to make you feel bad or to embarrass you in front of everyone here; it is to help you deepen understandings related to this critical question as both individuals and church leaders. Collectively, this could then, through you and others, help your faith community deepen theirs as well." Adam then looked over the group with a calm, reassuring smile that invited someone else to answer the question.

"I can try and answer the question, although I am pretty sure it will be wrong too," Audrey said in a somewhat haughty tone honed from practice. "It was, after all, what I was raised to believe by my parents, both of whom were looked up to as pillars not only of the church but of the community, and this was in great part due the fact that they were upstanding, moral Christians." Adam nodded for her to continue. "Well, simply put, I believe if you want to go to heaven, you must become a moral, upstanding person of character. My father was a stern disciplinarian, who didn't believe in spoiling the child by sparing the rod, and to be honest we had a healthy fear of him. Parents these days must be so careful about how they discipline their kids; even spanking for most parenting experts, and consequently many parents, is considered borderline abusive. Such lax parenting in my mind accounts for a lot of what's wrong with the younger generations today. Anyway, that's my understanding, God wants his children to behave." "I see," Ben followed up, "and exactly how do you see God's grace as factoring in here?" "Well," Audrey replied with a huff, "I don't claim to know exactly how God's grace works, but my father taught me to fear God and that God will reward us when we're good and punish us when we're bad. I always loved the verse that says, 'faith without works is dead,' although I couldn't tell you exactly where to find it in Scripture. I've always understood that verse to mean that those who live good and upstanding lives, worthy of the respect and admiration of others in the church and community, offer up the best proof that they are true Christians." "Actually," Pastor Jim interrupted, "what James was saying in his Epistle was if one has truly experienced God's transformative grace in Jesus Christ they are then empowered, by a reciprocating love and gratitude, through the Spirit to love God, themselves, and others in turn." Audrey, choosing to disregard Pastor Jim's instruction, and changing the subject, then said, "Besides, I was taught as a child that God decides ahead of time who will receive his grace, and by living exemplary, successful lives, we prove this to be true." "By golly, the woman sounds like a confused Calvinist, though she'd hardly be the first," Pastor Jim thought to himself. "Either way," Audrey persisted, "I don't think God dispenses grace to just anybody. I believe, at least to some extent, we must earn it." "Now she sounds like a semi-pelagian of a sort." His mind wandering in its habitual way Jim then recalled other theologians, both ancient and more contemporary, that he had read, or read about. He also recalled the affinity he had felt for the Dutch Reformer Jacob Arminius, who tried to reconcile free will with God's grace and omniscience. Then becoming suddenly aware of how obscure and unrelated such theologies were from the faith doubts and struggles of his parishioners, with a shake of his head, he subtly sniffed out a laugh to himself. Surely the profound writings of such Christian theologians were but intellectualized magnifications and further rationalizations of our very human tendency to try to understand something rationally that first and foremost must be subjectively experienced relationally with Jesus Christ. Even then, he thought, the ultimately unfathomable nature of how an infinite God manifested and bestowed His/Her grace on His finite human creation would always lie partly in the Divine realm beyond human comprehension. Jim smiled to himself as it occurred to him how easy it was, be it by theologians, philosophers, and others, to externalize, qualify, underestimate, distort, and institutionalize the radical nature of God's grace in Christ. Pastor Jim did have to concede that, as the apostle Paul alludes to in 2 Corinthians, there is such a thing as "cheap grace," where one thought they were saved by baptism or rite of Christian passage, without ever attempting to follow Christ.

Pastor Jim then heard Lynn begin to question Audrey, and it roused him out of his introspection. "Help me understand, Audrey," Lynn asked, "isn't grace something God gifts us redemptively upon our repentance and decision to accept Christ as our Lord and Savior? Aren't we then forgiven in spite of past transgressions and although we're still imperfect and may yet still stumble and fall? While I am not sure I believe this anymore, it seems to be more in accord with what the Gospels tell us about the radically inclusive grace of Christ. My older brother was a drug addict for years, and as most of the church knows he was arrested and spent time in jail before he surrendered his life to Christ. By your definition he wouldn't qualify as a Christian, much less make it into heaven." "Well," Audrey huffed, "I don't know about your brother, but I don't see how you can trust anyone who after sinning all those years suddenly then claims to be a Christian. It always seemed to me that once these wastrels had had their fill of fun in life, they then want the slate wiped clean and for God and everyone to forgive and accept them. Even if some of them appear sincere about their faith commitment, well, frankly I don't think a leopard can change its spots. Let me ask you a question. How in any way is that fair to those of us who have worked so hard to be good Christians for most or all our lives?" "I know my brother's history better than anyone here, and believe me he wouldn't describe addiction or what he went through as fun. I am guessing, Audrey," Lynn went on, "you're not familiar with Jesus' parable in Matthew 20 concerning the vineyard workers who arrived late in the day but were paid the same as those who had started working earlier?" "Honestly that story never made much sense to me, so I just ignored it." "I don't know, Audrey, but when you boil it all down it sounds to me like you're saying we must earn our way to heaven by being extra good?" Ben interjected. "As I recall, Audrey," Lynn said in a hurt and defensive tone of voice, "my brother got talked down a lot in the church due to his addiction and resulting lifestyle. Much of this, my grandmother, who used to quilt, told me originated with the quilting group you head." "And your question," Audrey snapped back. "Alright, let me try to ask you a more constructive question. Doesn't working so hard at being an upstanding, moral Christian make you resent anyone who doesn't try as hard as you, and can't this make you overly judgmental of others, particularly within the church?" "No one ever accused me of saying anything bad about that brother of yours," Audrey snapped back defensively. "That's because all those nasty things were said behind his and our family's back. All we kept hearing was 'you should know that people are saying bad things about your son or bad things about your brother.' When my parents or I would ask them which people, their answer was always that they had promised to keep their comments anonymous, but I just thought you should know what people are saying."

"Well," Audrey huffed, "people will talk, that's just human nature. I don't think there's anything wrong with someone saying what they see as the honest truth." "Honest truth, Audrey?" Pastor Jim repeated sarcastically. "I think you're confusing subjective opinion, to put it nicely, with little or no evidence to back it up, for some understanding of objective truth or fact. Gossip, which is what we're really talking about, seldom concerns itself with seeking out facts, much less constructive, resolution-oriented information about a situation or person. It most often involves tearing someone down anonymously, behind their back. In the end it is a highly dysfunctional way that people who feel weak and vulnerable, individually or collectively, compensate for by judging and attacking others while hiding behind anonymity. This often, particularly if they're part of a group participating in such behavior, can give them a false sense of superiority." Jim, who himself had been the target of such passive aggressive behavior, felt frustration and anger mounting within him but knew the current discussion was not the proper forum to vent any further. "Did you have a question for me, Pastor?" Audrey said curtly, taking advantage of his violation of the protocol. "Fair enough, here it is: Don't you think that such attacks go against God's law of love and on this basis alone would earn God's disapproval?" "Nobody is being attacked directly," Audrey responded, sounding quite sure of herself. "I agree with Williard, that such talk often serves a good purpose. If people couldn't remain anonymous, they could be attacked for what they're saying, and this would create even more tension and conflict." "The church is filled with conflict anyway," Pastor Jim responded in an exasperated tone, knowing that he and Audrey were slipping back into an argumentative mode, "and if we don't air our concerns in open, constructive ways, how will we ever resolve or get past these conflicts?" he said, looking at Audrey and then at Adam, pleadingly. Then looking directly at Audrey and in an exceedingly frustrated tone, he asked, "Audrey, have you never heard of passive aggressive behavior before?" When there was no response, he then followed this by saying, "Unfortunately many church groups and cliques have mastered this kind of aggression and become experts at it." Audrey met Pastor Jim's rebuke with a silent, icy stare.

Aware of the mounting tension Adam broke into the discussion and addressed the group. "I appreciate your efforts at trying to adhere to the question-answer format, but I am also aware how hard it is to set aside strong feelings, particularly this early in the discussion. I think Audrey has shared her answer to the question, as far as she understands it. Remember, we are all here to deepen our understanding of what it means to be a Christian. Strive once more, allowing for some discussion, to adhere to a question-and-answer format, and express yourselves in civil and constructive ways, and I think this will foster further reflection. Let us move on at this time. Who would like to share their understanding next?"

"Could I share a story first that might help us step back and see how most visitors and new members come to see a church filled with conflict, and I am sure much gossip and backbiting? It might also explain why so many of them don't stick around," Pastor Jim asked, turning toward Adam. "Go ahead, Jim," Adam responded patiently with a nod of his head. "My father had a pastor friend share an experience with him that my father then shared with me. In the early seventies this pastor had worked as a mediator in churches dealing with much internal conflict. When he arrived at the church where he was to act as a mediator, he entered the fellowship hall, and noticed that chairs had been placed in a big circle. With all opposing factions present, including the pastor of the church, the mediating pastor then led them in an invocation. After this he suggested they go around the circle and share their contentious perspectives regarding the church conflicts. The mediating pastor had hoped by doing this he might gain both a better sense of the differing views and collusions. He also hoped this would clear the air of much pent-up negative emotion. His instructions at the outset had been clear: 'Please no personal attacks, your remarks should be made as *I* statements, and keep your remarks to no more than three minutes each.' Despite this criterion, and before even one full circle of the participants was done sharing their views, the discussion format had broken down and had increasingly devolved into a free for all, with any semblance of civility abandoned. Despite the mediating pastor's best efforts at constructively refocusing the group, and deescalating the animosity, back and forth arguments, personal attacks, and name calling broke out again and again. As things devolved further and with participants increasingly talking over one another, the mediator realized he had totally lost control of the group. All chance of a constructive outcome appeared to have been lost.

"Then, just outside the basement windows of the fellowship hall, the loud revving of a motorcycle could be heard. A sudden curiosity on the part of all assembled caused the rancor to die down. All listened with anxious anticipation as heavy footsteps were heard descending down the stairs that led into the hall. As the double doors to the hall were pushed open, a collective gasp was heard. A tall, heavy-set full-bearded young man who appeared to be in his twenties appeared. He was clothed from head to foot in leather biking gear. Chains hung from his numerous pockets, with the longest chain hanging down from a hip pocket. Everyone in the circle looked to the mediating pastor to handle the alarming situation. His slightly upset but otherwise calm demeanor left them somewhat reassured and puzzled at the same time. All watched closely as the young man grabbed a chair and proceeded to make his way into the center of the large circle where he placed it and sat down facing the back of the chair. With everyone's eyes upon him he then took a few moments to stare back with a quiet intensity at everyone around the circle. A deep sigh of relief could be heard when the mediating pastor broke the silence. What had seemed like an unbearably long time had only been minutes. 'Bob, what are you doing here?' his tone and manner indicating that he knew the young man well. Slowly and with a big grin replacing the serious, slightly threatening look on his face, he replied. 'I just wanted to see how Christians act, Dad,' came the response."

Jim related that the son had heard his father was heading to mediate a particularly intense and divisive church conflict intervention and had decided to do an intervention of his own. "I am not sure if the father appreciated this, or how this affected the outcome of the meeting, but I think, as an illustration, this story makes an important point that we all need to hear. If this is how new members, those who visit us, and outsiders come to see us, it's no wonder they don't come around or stick around. Bottom line, nothing chases away potential members quicker than if they see us as a bunch of hypocrites who won't even try to practice what we preach. The worst thing for a church is not the occasional conflict it is bound to experience, it is the inability of its leadership and members to resolve those conflicts, and as the Lord taught us, to seek reconciliation. Why would anyone want to come to such a church? Already stressed by the times we live in and searching for acceptance and affirmation, wouldn't this be the last place they'd look?" "I don't think it has come to that at our church," Audrey muttered. "Be that as it may," Adam said, intervening, "I appreciate your sharing this story, Jim. No doubt we can all take something away from it. Perhaps more so as our discussion continues, and we reflect back on it." Adam then invited others to share their answers to the question at hand. An awkward silence followed yet again.

Then, surprising everyone, Fred entered the discussion. "Say what you like about how we appear to newcomers and outsiders; I can tell you that what closes the doors of a church quicker than anything else is when it runs out of money. Seeing what others have gone through, I am pretty sure whatever I say will not cut the mustard here, but I am going to say it anyway. I still think a financially solvent church is a healthy one that is more apt to survive. How can you expect the members of your church to maintain a strong faith if due to financial concerns they constantly must worry about whether their church is going to have to close its doors or merge with another church? There it is, and that's all I have to say, even if it doesn't answer your question," Fred said defiantly. "You really do need to add some fiber to your diet, Fred," Ben quipped sarcastically, then, catching Adam's gently disapproving stare, quickly apologized. Fred glowered resentfully at Ben.

"I have to say," Williard interjected, "I still believe that keeping the peace and defusing conflict wherever I see it arising is how Christ would have us act in the church." With everyone appearing a bit annoyed Williard lowered his head and diffidently added, "That's all I have to say for now." "So let me be clear, what you're reasserting, Williard, is that keeping the peace among Christians is the most important mission a Christian could have?" Jim said, summing up Williard's statement. "Yes, that's right," Williard replied enthusiastically, somehow mistaking Pastor Jim's restatement as an affirmation of what he had said. "But again, wouldn't you concede," Pastor Jim persisted "that by trying to defuse all the tensions you see arising in the church what you might be doing is allowing them to simmer on unresolved beneath the surface, creating even more division, misunderstanding, and tension, something I thought we'd explained before?" "I still feel that when Jesus taught that we should turn the other cheek, He meant just that. No matter what anyone says I don't believe that Christians should ever express anger toward one another," Williard added in a whiny, defensive tone. "And by the way, Pastor," he added, "I saw you get angry at a recent governing committee meeting, which did not set a good example for us. Pastors especially as men of the cloth should be setting a good example for the rest of us to follow. They should never express anger at their parishioners." "Williard," Pastor Jim instructed in a patient but weary tone as if he had explained this a hundred times before. "Jesus is teaching his disciples and us not to retaliate vindictively toward those who attack us, but rather, if necessary, with non-violent assertiveness and resistance where the ultimate goal is the correction and upbuilding of others. Make no mistake, though, even Jesus got impatient on occasion, even angry, both with his disciples and particularly with the Pharisees. I believe he called the latter a brood of vipers, among other caustic names. One other notable example was when he overturned the tables of the money changers in the temple. Once more Christ was both fully human and Divine in a way we can't fully comprehend. Being fully human he experienced every emotion we do. Remember, Williard, none of us, including pastors, stop being human just because we're Christians. If that were true, we wouldn't need God's grace." "Moreover," Lynn chimed in, "isn't the emotion of anger part of our createdness, and can't it even be a good thing if expressed in assertive, constructive ways?" "True enough, Lynn," Pastor Jim followed up. "Also, Jesus most often grew impatient or angry with those things that impeded His ministry and mission, particularly where it related to the marginalized, oppressed, and poor. His was more often a righteous anger that concerned itself with the welfare, spiritual and otherwise, of others." After pausing, Pastor Jim turned back toward Williard. "Don't you think, Williard, that you might be mistaking a hatred of confrontation and need to please everyone with keeping the peace?" Williard, who already appeared cowed by the critical feedback, lowered his head, feeling vulnerable and exposed.

"I for one, as you all know, get angry a lot about what's going on in this church," Ben said. "I am not defending Williard here, but I think others here, and not just Williard, are guilty of ignorantly cherry picking out Scripture texts that reinforce their errant beliefs and questionable Christian motivations. What Jesus wants most from us is a personal relationship with Him, wherein we allow ourselves to be transformed by His grace through the work of the Holy Spirit as we live out our faith in our daily lives," Ben expounded. "I am coming to accept that my anger is what stands between me and that relationship." Despite these reconciliatory comments Williard continued, with head lowered, to look utterly exposed and defeated. Ben, feeling a pang of sympathy for Williard, then said, "Williard, as Adam said, the goal here is not to invalidate your desire or ability to defuse situations, it is rather to have our motivations reprioritized and more constructively utilized as they are transformed by God's grace, and we align our will more with God's." "Please understand," Adam added in a reassuring tone as he looked around the circle, "what you're sharing may leave you feeling uncomfortable and vulnerable, but it is a crucial step if you want to grow as Christians and for your faith to provide you with the deeper, richer spiritual benefits it can offer."

"Well," Evelyn said abruptly, "I see where this is headed, and that is toward some fundy Christian understanding that does not conform at all with our tradition, where you must make some radical, once in a lifetime personal decision to follow Christ. I've heard that in some of these traditions they'll only baptize you as an adult, I guess that's so you're old enough to make this commitment on your own. I can't argue with their beliefs, each to their own, but I am pretty sure for their part they believe we're all going to hell if we don't believe exactly as they do." Pastor Jim responded in as calm and respectful a way as he could muster. "First off, I don't think Christ's desire for us to have a personal, lived out relationship with Him is the prerogative of any one church tradition, Evelyn. Perhaps we need to claim or reclaim and adapt some language from such traditions given their critical relevance for our tradition these days. Second, I am not sure the conservative Christian traditions to which you referred believe exactly what you just said. For those that might I don't think any church tradition is immune to all the ways we humans can, often unwittingly, substitute beliefs and institutional trappings for a deepening personal, organic, and passionately lived out relationship with Jesus Christ. To be fair, though, I am pretty sure that some extremely liberal traditions are as guilty of this as the very conservative ones."

Ben leaned in toward Lynn and whispered, "I think he's about to go off on another tangent. Watch, Evelyn's facial muscles will start to twitch. That'll be the tip off." "I know he does that a lot, but some of these tangents are related and informative," Lynn whispered back. Not hearing the exchange, Pastor Jim continued his digression. "In these traditions the beliefs of their adherents can make them just as prone to self righteousness. They too are liable to be wearing a false spiritual veneer which the unsuspecting will mistake for a profound, Christ-centered spirituality. Such Christians, at either extreme end of the spectrum, biblically and theologically have been among the most exclusionary and judgmental people I've known. They often condemn and hate associating with anyone who does not share their closed religious system of belief. Some of these Christian groups, be they liberal or conservative, are in danger of replacing a personal relationship with Jesus Christ with a very dogmatic set of religious, socio-religious, or politicized religious beliefs. This also makes it easier for them to claim that they speak for God. Their rigidly adhered-to religious belief system leaves little room for the awe, mystery, and humility that the Spirit of a transcendent God can invoke within us. We are reminded of this in 1 Corinthians 1 where Paul writes that God confounds those who boast of their wisdom to lift the weak and lowly. We must be careful not to unquestionably accept those who speak with a religious authority devoid of humility. Such conformist religious belief systems, be they extremely liberal or conservative, can be particularly deceptive substitutes for a living relationship with Jesus Christ."

Evelyn, who had been listening impatiently, made her annoyance apparent. "You've gone off on another tangent, Pastor. I had expressed my concern that you and Ben wanted us to become more like the fundies, particularly in relation to their beliefs in things like being born again and adult baptism. That is just not who we are. No surprise, but it doesn't matter," Evelyn scolded. "The fundies can believe what they like, we have our own way of ensuring that our children grow up to become Christians. This is why in infant baptism we believe the parents, the church, and God should all promise to help raise the child in the Christian faith, that is until confirmation where, if the pastor does his job right, they will be further educated, at the end of which they will be prepared to make their commitment to the church. That's precisely why we confirm them during the service. Their answers in the liturgical confirmation ceremony assures us of this."

"The problem is," Pastor Jim replied, "while that might have worked, to some extent, in bygone eras it's more complicated than that now. The current secular culture with its anti-Christian bias, along with the poor example many so-called Christian parents set for their kids, often make this rite a charade. The faith understandings of these preteens and teenagers are not adequate to withstand the assaults of a now proselytizing modern scientific worldview and the anti-Christian sentiment so pervasive in the culture. It is also questionable whether they are mature enough to even make such a faith commitment. Confirmation is the last place most of the kids I teach want to be. They are forced to be there by their parents as if baptism followed by confirmation are inoculations that will insure they'll go to heaven, or at the very least have some Christian values instilled along the way, however incoherently formed."

"Well," Evelyn huffed, unable or unwilling to hear or absorb any of what Pastor Jim had said, "and whose fault is that, perhaps if our pastor and church's leadership did a better job of modeling how Christians should act in our church, with reverence and a deep respect for our worship traditions, both these parents and their children would take confirmation more seriously." Ignoring Evelyn's accusation, Jim pontificated further. "What's important is that we find ways to validate their inner spiritual development and journey. This would mean that we should take any questions they might have at different developmental stages seriously. Neither should we put pressure on them to be confirmed by a certain age. The whole confirmation process needs to be revisited and re-envisioned. Perhaps some day within a more relaxed ecumenical framework the differing Christian traditions could share with each other still vital and relevant institutional and organizational traditions such as with youth ministries."

"He's off and running again, he's like a plane that doesn't know how to land," Ben whispered to Lynn. Oblivious, Jim pontificated on. "This might help our youth programs reach the youth wherever they might be at. Unfortunately, reactive entrenchment and clinging to outdated tradition, or at the other extreme watering down the faith to accommodate the culture, can stymie and stagnate spiritual growth. We can forget just how fallible human reason can be when adhering to rigidly held belief systems. I recently came across a study where those participants with the most set worldviews, religious or otherwise, felt they were correct 82 percent of the time. This doesn't leave much room for intellectual openness, much less humility." Having said this and realizing he was starting to run on again Jim paused, giving Adam a chance to redirect the discussion. "This discussion has been interesting, and insightful," Adam said, breaking in with a smile, "and understandable given your differing motivations as Christians. At this time, though, let us return to the question at hand."

At this Adam looked around the circle, once again welcoming others to share their answer to the question he raised at the outset: "What does it mean to each of you to say that you're a Christian?"

"Well, I am pretty sure my answer is going to be wrong too," Clark suddenly piped up, "but I'll give it a go. As you all know, I served my country honorably in the military." "Yes, Clark you've managed to work that into nearly every committee meeting discussion at some point," Ben sniped. Unfazed Clark continued, "It should be no surprise to anyone here, then, that for me being a Christian can be summed in five words: a love of God and country." "That would be six words, Clark," Ben sniped again. Clark paused, and with a furrowed brow and tilting his head to one side appeared to recount the words in his head. "Well, at least he's changed his motive from the one he gave during Old Pete's introductions," Ben whispered to Lynn. After pausing, Clark then continued. "When I was a child most people I knew believed as I do. Back then it was expected for teachers to say a prayer and then have us say the pledge of allegiance at the start of every school day. We need to bring that back. Taking prayer out of the schools limits our freedom of religion, something our country was founded on. Putting prayer and the pledge of allegiance back in the schools would be a great first step toward instilling better values in our children and making them better citizens. A love of God and country was something instilled in most children back then." "I think you might be a little confused here, Clark," Lynn interjected. "You're right that freedom of religion is every American's right, but our country's founders put that in the constitution to prevent our country from ever becoming a theocracy." "I think it's important to add here," Pastor Jim weighed in, "that Jesus couldn't have been clearer than in Mark 12:17 where He said, and I paraphrase, 'Give unto Caesar what is Caesar's and unto God what is God's.' He's clearly saying that the Christian faith should not be conflated with politics or nationalism." "And if I am not mistaken didn't Christ say that His kingdom was not of this world?" Ben chimed in. "Well, I may not know the Bible as well as you both," Clark snapped back defensively. "Or the constitution," Ben muttered derisively. Discounting what Jim and Ben had said, Clark continued, "Say what you like, what made this country great was a love of both God and country. After all, many patriotic Americans believe that God had a hand in establishing this country, and in one sermon our former pastor preached, he said that some of our country's earliest founders, the puritans and pilgrims, saw this country as a kind of new promised land. If true, wouldn't that make us God's new chosen people? What other country has done more to preserve freedom and democracy around the world," Clark concluded with a burst of enthusiasm.

"Oh boy, that's a minefield," Ben said under his breath. "That's a dangerous theology, Clark," Pastor Jim said weighing in, "as it conflates being a Christian with patriotism, and for reasons already given has no basis in Scripture. It can easily lead to some overzealous and exclusionary understanding of patriotism superseding faith as the primary motivation for being a Christian." "I think we might be getting pretty far afield," Ben interjected, "perhaps it's time we try once again to answer the question Adam initially posed to us." Adam, who had been listening patiently nodded approvingly.

After a long, awkward pause where no one seemed to want to go next, Ben, who had kept his head lowered at these times, slowly looked up at Adam and said, "I guess I could go next; I certainly have been sniping enough from the sidelines when I shouldn't have been in this discussion. This will involve some back history though." "Alright Ben, go ahead," Adam said encouragingly. "I know we're supposed to be posing questions that might help ourselves or someone else here clarify our thinking and reflect more deeply on the question at hand, so what I share here may sound like it's ignoring that guideline. Please know this is necessary to help you more fully understand both what being a Christian means to me, and why for me it remains an unlived truth. What follows is, in large part, my faith journey in recent years struggles and all.

"Also, some of what I am about to share will surprise most here. Some time after coming home from Iraq, I did take advantage of the GI bill to earn an associate degree from a community college in our area. By this time, I was a recovering alcoholic. While I had never done that well in school growing up, in college I found that I had an aptitude for philosophy and ethics, after taking courses in these areas and receiving top grades. This led me to read more on my own on related topics. Valuing faith, family, and friends above all else, I decided not to pursue further education and for a time took a series of jobs in construction. This left me free to spend more time on those things I was most invested in. I was never much into status anyway. Later, I would learn I had underestimated just how much some people are invested in worldly things like status and material and worldly success.

"Most of the deeper reflections and questions of faith I had were ones I wrestled with while I was in Iraq and afterward. These were further informed by long discussions I had with Pastor Jim in his office. On Saturday when I knew he was in his office I would call ahead and ask if I could stop by. Jim would respond cheerfully that it would offer him a welcome break from his sermon prep work. We would have these great discussions fueled by the two extra-large cups of coffee I would bring along. Pastor Jim helped me to approach my faith questions from a more sophisticated rational perspective. Please know, though, that while I thought it important to arrive at deeper faith insights in part by reasoning my way there, I never felt the need to rely on rational arguments alone. What I feel and experience in relation to my faith is equally important to me. Ironically, this aspect of my temperament may also be what's most responsible for my inability to renew my faith in God's saving grace.

"I have come to understand that to be a Christian one must have a lived out, personal relationship with God through Jesus Christ. It seems to me if that relationship was the greatest treasure in people's hearts, or at least what was most hoped for and sought after, this would be expressed in the way they live that faith out in their lives." "And what is faith to you, Ben?" Adam asked. "First and foremost, for me, it means being open to having a relationship with Jesus Christ, and I should add founded in an experience of His grace. To do this, though, you have to trust in the Lord and His promises, even if you still have some unanswered questions and doubts. If we have totally surrendered ourselves, or at least, those parts of us that stand between God and us, then our faith will truly be where our heart is and will also be our treasure." Ben paused, lowered his head, and as he raised it, sighed and said, "This can be hard to do, though, even if you have thought a lot about it and arrived at deeper understandings of what it means to live out your faith passionately in a relationship with Jesus Christ, as Pastor Jim and I have.

"The sad reality is we still have the free will, as Pastor Jim said, to choose not to trust the God we know in Jesus Christ. We too then just end up valuing something more than our faith in Christ," Ben admitted. "And what is it that you value more than your faith?" Adam asked gently. Ben's voice tightened a bit as if he had been sitting on pent-up emotion for a long time. "As I am sure you already know, it's the anger I hold inside.

There are lifelong members of this church who are familiar with many of the Bible's stories, have learned about Christ's teaching and mission, their faith tradition, and church institution, but I wonder if it ever even occurred to them to count the cost and make a real commitment to follow Christ into their everyday lives. In Mark 16 when the angel tells the women that the Lord has risen and will meet them in Galilee, he is telling them and us that we will find and experience Him in our everyday lives. I am no Bible expert, but during my tour of duty in Iraq, I read my Bible from front to back a few times and underlined many key passages. I wrote notes in the margins, particularly in the New Testament.

"There's nothing like being in the proverbial fox hole, although for me it was closer to the real thing, to cause you to either chuck your faith or explore it in a depth you never had before. I chose the latter path, and while I still have questions, I also arrived at a series of insights. Some of these came later with the help of an army chaplain, and more recently in talks with Pastor Jim. My faith deepened and became more profound. In Iraq I was forced to confront the stark reality of my mortality. I came to realize that the most essential preliminary choice we have in life is between trusting that there is some ultimate meaning and purpose to our lives, or that there isn't, with all the relativism and meaninglessness this implies. For that ultimate meaning to hold any personal, positively transformative relevance for us, we must be relationally significant to the ultimate author of that meaning and purpose which Scripture calls God. Having experienced the evil of war, I began to see God's omnipotent power to defeat human evil as obstructed by the fatal waywardness of human free will. I was taught as a child to believe that God's essence was love. I had seen evidence for this in the unconditional love my devout Christian grandmother had for me, and from those Christians who worked with me when I was a recovering alcoholic. Perhaps, though, I questioned, even Divine love has its limits. But I then asked myself, what greater love could that ultimate reality we call God show us than to come down among us as Jesus Christ and die, and then rise so that in His grace we might once again enter freely into a relationship with God? New questions, and doubts, then arose in my mind that convinced me that there are ultimately no conclusive rational or empirical proofs for either choice mentioned before, as we can prove neither that God exists nor does not. Nor can we prove or disprove that the universe is ultimately an arbitrary, meaningless, and authorless place. In the face of such ultimate rational uncertainty there may be a radical new sense of freedom. This, however, can also be under-ridden by a profound nameless angst.

Some seek consolation in the order reductionist materialism affords. This, however, mostly sidesteps the question of how and why everything exists. Many today arguing against the Christian faith, as Jim said earlier, assume the scientific method is the only way to prove something true. For me this is the height of human pride and arrogance. How can we know that when our minds, brains, and senses are so limited and fallible? There's so much we don't know about ourselves, much less the universe and reality, so much that we can't comprehend. To believe that the material world is all there is, and science is the only means by which we can understand reality and obtain truth, is to believe in nothing greater than ourselves. It is also to replace a worship of a transcendent God we can only know partly in Jesus Christ with a worship of reason that attributes an ultimate potential and value to itself in the form of a misapplied scientific method. Pastor Jim told me this is called scientism. This is so apparently questionable and dangerous. All we must do is ask ourselves how well this has worked out for us over the last hundred years since reason's enthronement. Two world wars, the threat of nuclear war, climate change, or in a medical context the ethical slippery slopes created by advances in areas like eugenics, and artificial intelligence. These offer just a sampling of some of the ethical slippery slopes created by our worship of human reason and belief that it is the culmination of human potential and social and cultural evolution. Plus, I worry that by restricting reality and truth to only the materialistic, empirical realm, this becomes self-fulfilling by assuming a hidden premise which rules out any non-materialistic evidence. Science as a method and tool has been and can be a blessing, but if mistaken for the ultimate truth it becomes dangerous and impoverishes the human spirit. Most would agree, just based on everyday life experience, that there are other ways to prove something true such as how ideas, values, and, yes, faith can improve and transform one's life both individually and collectively for the better. Unfortunately, our church is a bad example of this. So, for me once more that choice came down to choosing to live and die for something, rather than nothing, something that could be validated if I lived it as the greatest treasure of my heart. For me that something was Jesus Christ. My initial experience of God's loving grace enveloping my brokenness reassured me of its Divine source and power.

"After I came home from Iraq my faith may have been deeper, but it was still a fledgling faith. In Iraq I witnessed things I still have trouble talking about, and these contributed to faith doubts that continue to plague me. Soon after I got home, I married my first wife, someone I had grown up with in the church. This marriage failed due to reasons already given and others. After I turned my life around, I remarried and became active in the church again. It was then that my still formative new faith began to waver.

"My faith has really been challenged and tested by many of the church folk I've since encountered at the church. As I shared earlier some have treated me in a way devoid of any scriptural understanding of grace, others as if I was nothing more than my failures and work record. This helped fuel a growing anger within me. My wife keeps suggesting that we join another church, or denomination, but I keep reading about how the traditional denominations are in decline across the country. This makes me wonder if most of these churches and traditions don't, in varying degrees, share the same issues of overinvestment in the institution as does our church. I know this is overly cynical, and paints these churches and traditions with too broad a brush, but this is the way I mostly feel these days. So, as you might have guessed, I not only get angry, I also get depressed. Perhaps these are two sides of the same coin."

"Sounds like you're losing hope?" Adam responded. "Sometimes it feels like I have. Recently I read an article about the growing cultural phenomenon of the 'Nones,' the 28 percent of Americans who have broken away from institutional religion. The majority of these, while cutting ties with institutional religion, still claim to believe in God, question science's ability to explain everything, and still identify as being spiritual. Initially this reassured me that they haven't entirely given up the Ghost, no pun intended. The problem with those folk is that they've thrown the baby out with the bathwater. They won't even consider that time tested, healthier, and more relevant and evolved faith traditions and faith practices could still act as a guide for their faith development. It's one thing to temporarily lose your religion to regain your faith. It's another thing to permanently throw out the baby of still relevant, vital religious traditions with the bathwater of stagnant institutional church traditions that have become their own end. In any case, the vestiges of spirituality these so-called Nones might still have are no indicator of their long-term sustainability, much less of their return to any Christian fold. They become easy prey for vocal anti-Christian types and a new breed of angry, proselytizing atheists. Many of them sound like they have some kind of chip on their shoulder or hold some negatively unquestioned view of God. Why else would you get so worked up about something you claim doesn't exist and care nothing about?

"But then I read and hear about churches, or faith communities, in Africa, China, or South America, and how despite rampant poverty, and in many cases oppression, they are still thriving, and then I don't know. I also consider that the church in the West today, despite the obvious secular cultural tsunami, can't have it worse than the early church where there was often persecution and your life was often in danger just for being a Christian. So many oppressed people, slaves, women, the masses of poor people felt accepted and valued, often for the first time. The Good News of God's salvation is a timeless, transcendent revelation that can resonate with anyone who feels broken, marginalized, or seeks a deeper truth than this world can offer. So, I think to myself, if God could work in those times maybe He can work in ours as well. And so, you can see from all I've said how I go back and forth as I struggle to hang on to my faith and some hope for the church's future.

Ben suddenly grew quiet and lowered his head. "Ben," Pastor Jim said empathetically as Lynn put her arm around Ben, "sometimes it is only by acknowledging and confessing to the Lord the inner demons that possess us that His grace can fully heal us. I strongly suspect that is collectively the case with us here. Maybe, Ben, you need to trust the God you know in Jesus Christ with your anger." "I appreciate the thought Pastor, but I am not sure I know how to do that." "Have you tried sharing what that anger is hiding, all the shame, rejection, and hurt beneath it?" Not lifting his head, Ben responded, "I guess I am afraid I'll just be left with the anger and depression if I try to surrender them to God and He doesn't come through."

"Believe it or not Ben, despite key differences of what stands between God and us, I do understand how you feel," Pastor Jim followed up. "I have masked my faith doubts for so long by trying to rationally justify and explain my faith, that I worry that if I let go of this and try to surrender it to God and it doesn't work, I am not sure I'll be left with anything to shore my faith up, not to mention my call and ministry." Jim let out a deep sigh. "Like you I've thought, what if God doesn't come through?" Jim hung his head in despair.

"I don't know if this relates," Ben suddenly interjected, "but something a long-ago Christian mystic wrote, I must have read in college, just came to mind. It had something to do with learning to sit with thoughts and feelings of emptiness, and despair. He counseled that we should observe them with a detached prayerful mindfulness that entreats the Holy Spirit to fill the void we feel inside. Otherwise, he cautioned we might be tempted to fill it with worldly distractions and faith substitutes. I didn't hold the anger inside back then that I do now, so I couldn't see any life application benefit at the time." Ben then paused and scratching his head said, "I wonder what suddenly brought that to mind, maybe it was the beer." With that Ben sat back with something of a mystified expression.

"Thank you, Ben," Adam responded, "your recollection offers a key spiritual insight." Then turning back toward Jim, in a compassionate tone, Adam counseled him. "Perhaps you're mistaking uncertainties for faith doubts." Jim looked up with a questioning expression. "Forgive me, Adam, I am not sure I understand." "If you regard your faith doubts as potentially faith ending, I can see why you would hesitate to surrender them. What if, instead, you think of them as uncertainties that you ongoingly surrender to God in prayer? Perhaps then you might be provided with the hope and patience to live these questions, and the doubts they raise, until the answers arise from within with the help of the Holy Spirit. Remember too you might not be able or ready yet to understand or experience the answers God may have for you." "Thank you, Adam, that gives me some food for thought," Pastor Jim responded, raising his head and looking thoughtfully up at Adam. "Still though, I think it would be difficult for me to surrender all my doubts, my broken faith understandings, but perhaps gradually with the Holy Spirit's help I could prayerfully attempt this."

"How about you, Ben, could you surrender the hurt and pain you feel inside in this way gradually?" Pastor Jim asked, turning toward Ben. "I don't know, I sometimes feel like the Lord has led me right to the edge of a cliff where God is waiting on the other side with open arms promising to catch me if I leap. The chasm in between seems bottomless and contains all my fears, doubts, and failures along with all the substitutes for a living faith that can double as a defense against facing one's inner demons, like my anger. Then at the last possible moment, I back away from that cliff's edge. I have done this over and again. I don't think this is what you mean by gradually surrendering my hurt and pain. Since becoming active again in the church I am having trouble trusting that God is really there, or that there is such a thing as Divine grace that could heal someone as broken as me." With that Ben paused, lowered and then raised his head, and after a deep sigh spoke again.

"Well, I can honestly say what I said before is the most, outside of my wife, I've shared about myself and my faith with anyone. This normally doesn't come easily for me. It's like a dam burst inside of me." Then for levity Ben grabbed a tankard and added with a sheepish grin, "Maybe it is the beer. In any case Pastor Jim, you've got competition." Surprisingly, though most there were now reclining back in their chairs, far from appearing bored, they were once more focused intensely on Ben. The astonished looks on their faces no doubt were due to the depth of personal reflections that they had not thought Ben capable of. For Pastor Jim and Lynn this had not come as a surprise.

"You say you've gained insights from me Ben, and I hate to lower your estimation of me, but I must remind you again: all these insights are intellectual. I too worry, as I said, albeit for different reasons, whether God will catch me if I take that leap you just talked about. Like you, I go back and forth in my head debating reasons both for and against putting my faith in the God I know in Jesus Christ. I am just beginning to trust more, though, that while God allows us the free will to make such a leap, He is present with us at that precipice ready to guide and empower us. Not long ago, I did finally conclude that reason and rational proofs for God's existence will not preserve what little of my faith remains. In fact, as it turns out, they may be the primary thing in my chasm that I must leap over.

"If God is infinitely greater than I can imagine, then there is no way reason alone could fathom how an infinite God became human much less how that could bring something finite, us, back up into an eternal relationship with Him. There is a paradox here that reason alone cannot resolve. Perhaps, I tell myself, the truest test of faith and of being a Christian then is daring to live out that faith, trusting that God's faithfulness will bear out.

Maybe this is, at least in part, and despite uncertainty, what we should be leaping toward. Maybe the proof I am looking for only becomes more evident as I open my heart and mind to God, and I am enabled, through the power of the Holy Spirit, to better understand God's purpose and meaning in my everyday life. What if choosing to make that, in part, non-rational leap is the only way to overcome this paradox? I mean, my doubts and endless attempts to rationally prove God's existence have only left me unfulfilled, restless, and in despair. A part of me, deep down, intuits that I am more than a finite physical being. That part of me slips into a life-negating despair when for any length of time I try to suppress the eternal part of me that desires a relationship with the Divine. Most recently I am coming to see, due to my experience here, that the only antidote for this deep, soulful undercurrent of despair is to live out my faith in a personal relationship with Christ. I've tried to will myself to trust that God's transformative power and faithfulness will bear out. But trying to will oneself to trust God, as you might gather, becomes just another way to not trust God.

"My fear of surrendering my rationales for faith, as with your anger, still holds me back. Sometimes I worry that all my studies in both college and seminary, rather than helping to preserve my faith, have become the biggest stumbling block to my ability to trust that Christ is truly what our faith claims Him to be. The Lord taught us that we must have faith like a child. That was an understandable teaching given the crowds that came to hear Jesus preach. I don't know if that is possible anymore for me, and I dare say for many in our culture these days. I resonate strongly with that often-heard refrain of many Christians who have fallen away from going to church; 'I just couldn't keep checking my brain at the church door anymore.' I tell myself that the Holy Spirit will meet me where I am at and take all this learning and put it into a deeper and more profound, Christ-centered context. But then I recall what Paul wrote in 1 Corinthians, something about God choosing to use what the world looks upon as foolish to shame the wise. Having said this, I don't confuse what Christ meant when He exhorted us to have a faith like a child's with that of a childish faith. A childlike faith stems from the humility, joy, awe, and mystery faith can instill in us, the latter from spiritual immaturity.

"I've also told myself, rather than asking why the ultimate reality we call God would come among His wayward, primitive human creation, we should consider that it is precisely because of His unfathomable love and power that God was able to break into our worldly realm in human form.

And just maybe we humans needed His sacrificial Divine intervention to repair the breach created by a willful and wayward humanity, however you want to understand original sin. More positively, I tell myself, discounting those through history who were Christians in name only, much good has been done by those who truly sought to love God and others as Christ did. This is evident in our literature, our art, our legal system, in our ideals such as our evolving understandings of equality, in our social programs, and so much more.

"Of late, while these back-and-forth conversations within me have increased, and despite the profound new insights I've gained, I still have trouble letting go of all my doubts. I am sure that all that science has taught me, in school and beyond, about this world and the universe is reinforcing these doubts as well." "Don't forget, Jim," Adam said in a gently persuasive way, "that some of the greatest and most renowned scientists and philosophers, today and through history, not to mention faith-informed biblical scholars, believe this simpler, more straightforward understanding of Scripture. It is precisely because of their learning and profound insights and understandings, and not by setting their learning aside, that they arrived at their profound faith convictions." "I know what you're saying is true Adam, and yet still, despite all you've said, I have trouble trusting the Lord with my doubts and need to rationally justify my faith."

"I hear you Pastor," Lynn suddenly said in a tone that exposed something of her own inner doubts. "What Adam just said rings true, but I too have been unable to make such a faith leap, and it is precisely because of the way both Ben and you have described it. It's so radical, so trusting. In the end that faith leap still requires me to, well, make a leap of faith. Faith just seems so out of step with the cynical, materialistic times we're living in, plus the leap Ben spoke of sounds like it would demand a blind faith from us. I've read and heard about too many religious nuts who evidenced that kind of blind faith." "Despite all my doubts Lynn," Pastor Jim instructed, "I don't share your concern here, and I'll tell you why. Recall again Christ's law of love, and His greatest commandment 'to love the Lord your God with all your heart, with all your soul, and with all your mind, and the second . . . you shall love your neighbor as yourself.' This is the lens through which all religious law, tradition, and scriptural texts should be understood and interpreted. I think this offers a critical framework and context to your concern about blind faith. Jesus is clearly telling us, in light of the cross, that what we're making a commitment to, first and foremost, is the radically inclusive, liberating power of God's grace. The Holy Spirit gifts us then with the eyes and ears of faith and calls forth from us a passion to love God in turn, and share that love with others. Moreover, God gifted us with a reasoning brain, not to solve all our problems without God's help, but to see how best to express this love, with the empowerment of God's Spirit, within a given context. I see Christ's greatest commandment as the tallest peak of Scripture where, looking down from its lofty height, we gain an essential perspective on the rest of Scripture, Christian tradition, and our lived out faith lives.

"If I were to make that leap while prayerfully keeping the greatest teaching of Christ's in heart and mind, I think it would keep me humble and open to further growth spiritually. Understanding Jesus' mission and ministry in light of His greatest commandment would also hopefully help me resist the temptation to corrupt the faith for selfish and worldly purposes. One valuable insight I've gained from my reflections is that, while I might journey toward an increasing awareness of God's greater plan for me and this world, as a fallible human being, it will always remain beyond my comprehension and ability to fully grasp. Sorry, I've fallen yet again into a lecturing mode, but perhaps something of what Ben, Lynn, and I have shared of our faith struggles and reflections will be of help to others here."

There was a long pause as Adam looked in turn at Ben, Jim, and Lynn appreciatively. Finally with an approving nod of his head, he broke the silence. "I have heard some of you talk of your past, and how certain formative experiences contributed to the hurt and insecurities you hold inside. You also seem somewhat aware of the defenses you've developed that suppress both. In addition, you have shared how all this has contributed to your respective faith doubts. You also seem more aware that it is only by trusting that God's saving grace in Christ is real and has the power to heal your brokenness that its truth becomes your truth from the inside out, in body, mind, and soul. This insight can lead to a deeper understanding individually and collectively of what it means to be a Christian. At the deepest level there is an anxiety all human beings share when considering the leap Ben spoke of; can I prayerfully trust the God I know in Jesus Christ to grant me the grace and courage to live my faith, despite uncertainty, in a way that fulfills my deepest needs for meaning and affirmation in and of my life? This anxiety shadows the lives of those who hedge their bets against trusting God more fully in Christ, by investing themselves in the worldly externals of pleasure and materialism. For those invested in the institutional church this often takes the form of mere religious observance or adherence.

"Still, while these doubts and investments may well be holding you back from making the leap of faith Ben talked of, I think there is something else as well that is holding you back. Something that so far has not seemed to play a major or vital role in helping you resolve your faith doubts, despite your occasional references to it. You seem to be somewhat aware that the Holy Spirit has assisted you on your faith journey to that precipice. You also seem somewhat aware that that Spirit can also assist you both in your decision and in the act of making that leap of faith, as well as on your continuing journey after having made this radical leap of faith. But what is easy to underappreciate and forget is that it is only through the conduit and life centered practice of prayer that we become fully aware that the Holy Spirit is at work in our life. The wonderful thing about prayer is that even if you have never known the Lord, or have lost your way, when you cry out to the Lord with an honest and open heart, you are more apt to hear and experience His answer and presence. You may also in unique circumstances enable others to do the same. Your pastor cried out to the Lord three times: once before he planned this retreat, then while on the bus, and finally on a desolate road on his way here. Pastor Jim was open and receptive to hearing and receiving the answer given.

"It is the nature of God's agape love that you are left free to make that leap of faith, but within that freedom is a more subtle freedom, the freedom to pray for the comfort, guidance, and empowerment of the Holy Spirit before, during, and after that leap. Having made that leap of faith the Holy Spirit, particularly in a prayer-centered faith life, will continue to accompany you wherever your faith journey and God's plan for your life takes you. That same Spirit will counsel and inspire you as your faith continues to grow in an understanding of God's word. It can also work through the truly grace-filled fellowship of those who are sustained by that Spirit to live out his word in light of our Lord's greatest commandment.

"You see, an active and passionate relationship with the living Christ depends more on a prayer-centered faith life than you can imagine. Consider how one's family life and relationships would suffer without any open or honest lines of communication. What then do you think would happen to your relationship with God without such communication? I realize many reduce prayer to either the rote prayers said in church, before meals, and other traditionally prescribed occasions, or more spontaneously at times of great need for yourselves and others, such as during illness. A deeper understanding of prayer underlies these and all the forms prayer can take. The prayers your Father in heaven longs most to hear are those from the heart. Those prayers are meant to be part of an ongoing conversation between God and His human creation, and children whom He dearly loves. Think of those adult children who call or visit their parents infrequently more out of a sense of duty or need than motivated by love and a desire for a closer relationship. Perhaps some of you have experienced this, but if not imagine how this would make you feel. In God's creation plan He instilled within you an innate capacity and longing, along with a free will, for a personal relationship with Him. This, then, is the indispensable means and conduit by which that relationship is initiated, maintained, and sustained with the assistance of the Holy Spirit."

Adam then paused to let what he had just said sink in. One could hear a pin drop in the silence that followed. The silence was finally broken by Pastor Jim. "The importance of prayer was instilled in me by my parents from little on up, at mealtimes, bedtimes, for those in need. Since college I have increasingly spent so much time in my head rationally trying to reassure myself of God's existence that I totally neglected a genuine prayer-centered faith life." Lynn jumped in, saying, "Me too Pastor, although for a different reason. Having grown up in and forced to go to our very traditional church every Sunday, I was so sick and tired of saying the same old rote prayers. They no longer held any meaning for me. Then the way the congregation would drone on through the prayers and liturgy with a lack of vitality, passion, or any awareness that they were supposed to be connecting to the living God we know in Jesus Christ, well, let's just say it didn't help. Hymns were often sung, except maybe on the holidays, in the same way. That many of these prayers, not to mention the liturgy and hymns, relied almost exclusively on antiquated religious language that did not speak to many of my generation didn't help either. Consequently, by the time I was a young adult, when it came to prayer, I was thoroughly convinced that this was all prayer amounted to. Much later I briefly attended a more conservative church's worship service with a college friend and was shocked to see, even though I didn't share all their beliefs, the passion with which they sang, read Scripture, and prayed." "I can relate to that, Lynn," Ben said. "I too had put my prayer life on a back burner, although for different reasons. I had an active prayer life in Iraq, but when I came home and was once again involved in the life of the church, my prayer life faltered. It just didn't seem like my prayers for my fellow church members to come to know the living Christ were having any effect. I am finally beginning to realize that what I should have been praying for was myself, for all the hurt, low self-esteem, and anger within me I have suppressed and denied for so long. We often forget that we can't love others, or even God as we should, if we don't allow ourselves to experience and be nurtured into self-love through God's saving grace."

"Prayer," Adam said in a gentle, compassionate way, "is not first and foremost about changing God, or even our life circumstances. Prayer is about allowing God, through the work of the Spirit, to change and ultimately transform the way we look at ourselves, other people, and the world, especially as it regards life's greatest joys and troubles. Please know, though, that God can and does intervene in your lives and the world in ways that often seem mysterious and beyond our ability to rationally understand at times. But again, God seeks to establish a saving, and grace-filled, relationship with every one of you. Prayer is essential then to both the establishing and continuance of this relationship so that you might be transformed and see the world anew through the eyes and ears of faith."

After Adam stopped speaking another pregnant pause followed. Lynn broke the silence. "What you, Pastor, Ben, and now Adam have shared is helping me to arrive at deeper insights regarding my faith life. Although, probably like the rest of you, my mind is reeling with all I have heard and am trying to process. What Adam just shared, though, has put a missing piece of the puzzle into place for me. I've just gotten so used to thinking that God needed our help that I neglected to trust in the power of a prayer-centered life to sustain my faith. I couldn't conceive of and became closed to the possibility that God's plan for the church, the world, and me might be much greater than anything I could conceive of, and that nevertheless running through all of it is God's Divine, saving Love. It now occurs to me that God has not abandoned us, allowing the church and faith to die, but rather God is pruning back the dead branches off the main vine, which will be our true lifeline for whatever form or forms the faith, and the community of faith, we presently call the church will take in the future."

"Do you recall from an earlier discussion what the earliest church was called?" Adam then asked, directing the question to all there. "Wasn't it the Way?" Ben answered. He then looked at Adam and asked a question in turn. "So, is being a Christian more of a verb than a noun, and not just for individuals, but for that community of faith we call the church?" After pausing briefly Ben went on to answer his own question. "Perhaps, then, by prayerfully fulfilling our potential through God in Christ's Spirit, we might better stay the course made mindful of our Lord's greatest commandment. This in turn might help us see more clearly why a rigid and static adherence to some dogmatic or institutional understanding of what it means to be a Christian can be so misguided. Hasn't it been an investment in the latter that has led many to see being a Christian more as a noun than a verb, more about being identified as a mere adherent to a set of beliefs and traditions than a lived out faith?" Ben had said this with a degree of growing self-satisfaction. "Maybe it is only when we approach the cliff's edge having prayerfully sought God's radically inclusive, healing grace, despite uncertainty, that the Holy Spirit can most fully empower us to make that leap, our prayer-centered life gradually awakening us to all that stands between us and God.

"Perhaps without fully realizing it I saw sin primarily as a list of moral failures, rather than as all that separates from God's saving love, including my anger. I bet my anger was a good part of what is in that chasm I need to leap across," Ben said with a burst of enthusiasm. "You're on a roll Ben, careful you don't hurt yourself." Lynn teased affectionately.

I think it follows," Lynn added, "if I understand what Adam and others have said about living out Christ's law of love more passionately and prayerfully, that perhaps I've been overly assertive at times in ways not grounded in that love." "That's an understatement," Wes could be heard mumbling. "I have a question," Lynn then asked, "and it may sound a bit ignorant and naïve. Does that mean, and please know I don't want to sound like Williard, that I can no longer be assertively confrontational about those issues I care most about?" "Do I really sound that bad?" Williard whined to Scott sitting next to him. Lynn had directed this question toward Adam. "What have the Scriptures taught you about this?" Adam asked in turn. "Well, from what I recall, and what we discussed earlier, Christ did seem to get angry with the Pharisees a lot. But this anger was more often one of righteous indignation, particularly when directed toward the Pharisees, whose self-righteous religious legalism was further oppressing an already oppressed people." "He got angry at other times too, Lynn," Ben interjected. "He got frustrated with his disciples and followers too, especially preceding that last trip to Jerusalem. He knew how critical the fulfillment of His mission was, in the end, to their salvation and their faith in Him. That might have been righteous indignation too, but I bet there were times the disciples just plain annoyed the fully human side of Him." "What I am learning here," Lynn then went on, "is that when I am assertive and confrontational, while not suppressing my anger and frustration, the goal I should strive toward prayerfully is the building up and edification of another's faith, something Paul wrote about in one of his letters to the Corinthians, that I knew about but chose to ignore." "I think Jesus' teaching to first examine the log in our own eye before judging another might be relevant here as well," Pastor Jim then interjected. "Ouch," Lynn said, "that's another one I've chosen to ignore."

"Given that you are human," Adam then continued, "and this extends to pastors as well, you are bound to express anger in negative ways at times. It is important, lest you let that anger possess you in destructive ways, that you confess it to the Lord with a prayerful heart that seeks continually to be recentered in God's love and grace. The unbroken channel Christ had with the Godhead was anchored in the prayer life He modeled for us, and ensured that He would not abandon that relationship or His ministry and mission. Something, being human, one can only aspire to through the grace God affords." "So, I guess that leaves me plenty of room to be more constructively assertive," Lynn said in a self-reassuring way. "I had assured myself all this time that I was angry at church members for not pulling their weight to help God bring in His kingdom, and that my anger was more like righteous indignation, but I am beginning to see that it's God I've been most angry at for letting His church down, and not saving it. Deep down, as I alluded to earlier, I had begun to wonder if God had just given up on us, or if there even was a God. I can more clearly see now that while God doesn't need me to save the faith and church for Him, the God who in Jesus Christ seeks to be in a relationship with me does want to work in and through me. I am beginning to understand now that the passion and motivation for this is very different from what I thought it was. I think without realizing it, by doubting God's greater plan, I had bought into a kind of works-righteousness. The part of me that was still hoping God was there was nevertheless trying to prove that we were worth saving, just in case God had turned His back on us. I can see now that both my motivation and passion for living out my faith must stem from and be sustained by ongoing experiences of that grace, and not by treating it as a reward for filling in for God. Thanks to Adam I am also coming to see how critical prayer is to a grace centered life." Lynn then grew quiet, her thoughts turning inward.

Looking around the circle Adam then began to speak again. "Some of you have remained quiet," he noted in his gentle, patient way. "Would you like to add anything to the discussion at this time?" Another long pause followed in which shoe shuffling, coughs, and other sounds could be heard that conveyed the nervous tension around the circle. Despite the silence Adam waited calmly. Pastor Jim broke the silence. "I do have one question for Adam that I think has been on most of our minds. Is the experience we're all having a kind of purgatory? Some of us, or at least I, wanted to ask this from the outset of our time here but I think I was too afraid to hear the answer." Adam smiled knowingly. "I was expecting someone to ask me that, so let me answer, no, you are not in purgatory, or some halfway house between heaven and hell. What you all are having is a unique experience meant only for those gathered here. In part it was an answer to the prayers of desperation your pastor made both for himself and on behalf of all of you. I will not tell you more right now, but as you journey on it will become clearer why Pastor Jim and the rest of you are having this shared experience." "Still, it all seems a bit mysterious," Pastor Jim said. "If we ever wake up from this experience, assuming we weren't killed in the collision, I plan to write about it and share it with both with my church members and perhaps others." After saying this, Pastor Jim grew quiet and appeared lost in thought. "I want to thank Jim, Ben, and Lynn for all that you've shared," Adam interjected. "Some here may find it very helpful and it could lead to deeper insights and understandings of what being a Christian is most essentially about."

Williard, surprising everyone, suddenly spoke out. "I resonated with much that Pastor Jim, Ben, and Adam have shared. What Ben said about the cliff, and Pastor Jim said about living a more passionate faith life, and what Adam said about the central importance of prayer to a lived faith really got me thinking. You did too, Lynn. I never stopped to consider that God's plan for me and the church may be much greater than I could imagine. It may feel like a huge gamble, but as Adam, or someone, said, we're not even alone at the very edge of that cliff, and prayer can make us aware of the Holy Spirit's presence there with us. I am beginning to see how superficial and misguided my understanding of what being a Christian was all about. I can now see that to go from those misunderstandings to one where I am living out my faith prayerfully in a Christ-centered way might require a leap of faith, a leap where we must open ourselves to an experience of God's grace, especially regarding those parts of us that need that love most.

"I resonated with Ben's leap analogy, but one thing still confuses me. To make that leap wouldn't we have to deny and leave behind the very parts of ourselves which we most need to bring with us into the loving embrace of God's grace on the other side of the chasm? If we're just jumping over all that, how does that lead to God's grace empowering us to accept, heal, and integrate these parts of ourselves into a greater and healthier sense of self?" "The leap analogy," Pastor Jim instructed, "was originally alluded to by a Danish philosopher and theologian named Kierkegaard. I must have shared something about this with Ben in one of our many in-office conversations. For Kierkegaard this signified a leap over externalized religion and any rational attempt to prove one's faith. I don't think the leap Ben refers to means exactly this. Having said that, neither do I think Ben means that we should ignore or deny those parts of ourselves but to prayerfully do some soul searching so we honestly confess them to God, abetted by the Holy Spirit. Let me see if I can extend this to Ben's leap analogy.

"Correct me if I am wrong Ben, but in your understanding the chasm represents not only the endless rational and externalized proofs for God in Christ that I sought after, but all those parts of ourselves we don't trust God with. This includes, among many other things, insecurities, failures, a deeper need for meaning and purpose in our lives, and our fear of mortality. The leap, then, is toward trusting that through God's grace they might be integrated into a more authentic sense of self in Christ. Much of what's in that chasm depends on where we are on our faith journey and our life circumstances at the time." "You're doing fine, Pastor," Ben interjected. "In fact, you're extending the analogy beyond where I had gotten with it, and I like where you're going with it." Pastor Jim smiled back at Ben and replied, "Well, then let me keep extending it. Many may well have to jump over numerous chasms in their lives contingent on such factors. Although close Christian friends of mine have shared that the first time they made such a faith decision, or leap, their experience of God's loving grace in Christ God reinforced and validated the wavering trust they felt before. This in turn made it easier if they felt they had to make that decision or leap again. Maybe then it's only when we prayerfully surrender whatever stands between us and God, over and again, if need be, that we provide God's loving grace the greatest opportunity to gradually transform us, helping us accept all that we are and can be in the light of God's healing love. We shouldn't forget, though, that this leap of faith over a chasm is still only an analogy and cannot do justice to the faith process of surrendering all that we are, even if piecemeal at times, into God's loving arms."

Williard had been listening intently to the exchanges between Ben and Pastor Jim. Adam once more broke into the discussion. "Again, what Pastor Jim and Ben had to say may prove very beneficial to some here, but now I would like to hear more from Williard." Williard, picking up from where he had left off, said, "I didn't say all that just to please Ben, Pastor Jim, Lynn, or you Adam, I really think that most of us here thought that serving the institutional church was the default setting for what it meant to be a Christian. I'd like to blame this on the way we were raised, and how our elders modeled this for us, but most of us know the Bible well enough, have attended enough Bible studies, and listened to enough sermons over the years, that we should have been able to arrive at some deeper understanding of what it means to be a Christian. I guess what it says in Scripture is true, that you need the eyes and ears of faith to be able to see and hear God's word and begin to understand it. What Adam and Pastor Jim alluded to makes sense to me now, that such a decision or leap of faith can be empowered by the Holy spirit, before, during, and after we have made that leap. I have to say I don't know if it's the bread and beer, Adam, or some of you here, but my experience here is shaping up to be the greatest, and maybe the only real, spiritual awakening of my life. That cliff Ben talked about, even if only an analogy, suddenly feels real to me, and I find myself at the edge of it perhaps for the first time, counting the cost, as Jesus taught, and considering whether to leap or not.

"If I am brutally honest with myself and you all here, trying all this time to please everyone has been exhausting, and while some might like me because they find me so agreeable, most people as they get to know me seem to lose respect for me, and that hurts, really hurts. Strange isn't it, the very thing I thought I wanted all this time, to be liked and accepted, now that I think about it, wasn't what I really wanted at all. What I really wanted, deep down, was to be loved and respected for who I truly am. Something God, and those who have known the amazing, transformative power of His grace, could offer me. In the end I now think this would be enough. Going all the way back to my school days, I always felt like the odd man out, like I didn't belong or fit in. Perhaps this was due to my more sensitive nature and the fact that I didn't like doing a lot of the things the other boys were into. I've tried to deny these insecurities my whole life, but inside I felt weak, different, vulnerable, and that I didn't belong. It didn't help that I was always small for my age, skinny, and wore thick, black-framed glasses often held together in the middle by adhesive tape."

Williard paused, realizing that everyone was staring at him, including Wes and Clark, and were having trouble believing what was coming out of his mouth. Most wore looks of astonishment as if to say, Is this same Williard we've known for so long who hardly ever says anything that seems genuine and forthright? Pausing for a moment, Williard quietly looked back at all the faces around the circle. He felt unburdened and more authentically himself than he ever had before. A quiet calm came over him, and he began to speak again. "So, there you have it, in short, I am really a nerdy, little, insecure man who's been a total fraud for a long time, but I also feel ready, for the first time, to trust all that baggage with the God I want to know in Jesus Christ. Even though I know the cliff analogy has its limitations, I still find it helpful. I am also beginning to understand that leaping over all that insecurity doesn't mean denying it, but rather mindfully and prayerfully leaping over my need to build defenses around it all. Like Ben I always thought sin was what we did wrong, what was immoral; I am now beginning to see that it can be seen as anything that separates us from God's love in Christ, including our fears and insecurities, and vanities." "I know you've been holding in a lot of hurt, shame, and other emotions," Adam said empathetically.

"Yes, I can now see," Williard answered, "by trying to win everyone's approval, what I was really doing was trying to pacify and suppress those feelings. I am also beginning to understand how through God's love and grace I could become a stronger, more authentic person, and most important of all a better Christian. I bet too that my faith will deepen as I prayerfully strive to live it out. I know one thing for sure, and that is I will no longer associate being a Christian with the role I played in the church, totally disconnected from a lived out faith. Anyway, that's it for me, sorry if I overshared."

Williard felt a quiet confidence rising within him. He thought to himself, "Even if some of these people here think even less of me than they did before, at least I can stop pretending to be something I am not and let go of that exhausting need to please everyone. I can start being just myself. Besides then I might finally be able to tell who really likes and cares about me, God included, if tempted as I am to make that leap."

"Thank you, Williard," Adam said. Then, by way of acknowledging the stunned silence that followed Williard's further confessions and reflections, he added, "What Williard just shared was from the heart. Trust me, God knows the content of your heart even when you deny or suppress it. As unnatural and vulnerable as it might make you feel, it is when you confessionally share your innermost thoughts and feelings with God, and at appropriate times with others in Christ, that God's healing, transformative love and grace can be brought fully to bear. Is there anyone else here who would like to speak?" "But isn't our awakening to what stands between us and God most often a process?" Ben asked, interrupting Adam. "And what if that part of us is mostly unconscious, how do we become more aware of it?" "That's why, once again, a prayer-centered faith life is so critical," Adam responded. "It is primarily through a daily prayer practice where we share our deepest emotions, doubts, and reflections that the Holy Spirit will help us expose those parts of ourselves to God's healing grace. This does not mean that confessional prayer is all that our prayer life consists of. Prayer, after all, is most essentially a conversation with God. Many names have been given to the different forms that conversation takes, but in a life centered around a relationship with Christ, and His word, prayer becomes a natural, flowing conversation despite its many aspects. Although once understood, this understanding of prayer can benefit from the worshipful discipline that uses a variety of prayer forms."

Adam then became quiet and cast an expectant look about the circle. Another long pause followed. Adam, who seemed as comfortable during these awkward silences as he did at any other time, looked about the circle again, conveying patience and empathy. He made no attempt to fill the silence with instruction or judgment but waited patiently until someone felt compelled to speak up. Finally, after what seemed like forever, Wes cleared his throat and started to speak.

"Contrary to what you might think, I have been listening to everything that's been said, and what Williard just shared caught me off guard. After the initial shock wore off, I started thinking. I have to say it made me reflect on my understanding of why I do the work I do for the church. I am also beginning to understand, or for the first time want to understand, where this motivation came from. My father was a man's man, one of those guys that other guys just naturally respect and follow. He had served in World War Two and been awarded numerous medals, the Purple Heart, bronze medal, and others. He reached the rank of colonel, and most in town including a lot of my friends referred to him as that. He wasn't an emotional guy and had a hard time expressing his love for his children, me included. He also demanded much from us, particularly my brother and me, and had little tolerance for what he saw as weakness, crying, wanting sympathy, not standing up for yourself, that sort of thing. Still, as I grew up, I wanted nothing more than to be like him. Almost everything I did, I did with a mind to make him proud of me. He never talked much about his service during the war. We all knew that he saw and probably had to do some awful things fighting against the Japanese in the Pacific. Two of the things he stressed a lot were the importance of getting the job done and one's duty. He often fell back on military jargon, reminding us of the importance of completing whatever mission we were tasked with, along with doing one's duty and preserving one's honor. He passed away some years ago, but I think of him often. Much of what I have tried to succeed at as an adult, I am beginning to see, has been an attempt to win his approval. Even since he passed, I am still trying to win that approval. Deep down I never thought I could be the man he was; I wasn't as strong, as masculine, even though some might see me that way. If I am honest, I can now see that what I've really been striving for all this time was not just his approval but his love. He never actually told me he loved me, you know." Wes's voice cracked a bit as he said this. "I'd have given almost anything just for him to have said this to me once. The most he ever did was shake my hand firmly and say, 'good job,' if I did something right. I guess the way I managed my employees and subcontractors all these years became a primary way of seeking his approval. After all, it was all about completing a mission and being told you did a good job by a superior. I also loved overseeing others and telling them what to do, something he was good at. Unlike him, I've tended to look down on those beneath me, and associated dominance with strength. Again, deep down I think I was projecting the weakness I feared was inside of me onto others."

Meanwhile Alice was now staring at Wes with her mouth wide open in disbelief. "Who is saying this," she thought to herself, "it can't be Wes, my closest ally at the church, especially regarding matters pertaining to the building? What was this place doing to people? Was it the beer, the bread, Old Pete, Adam, or the overall effect of the place? What might it do to me if I stay here long enough?" She shook herself slightly as if to shake off any effect the place might be having on her. "Hopefully," she reassured herself, "this is all just a weird, albeit very real seeming, dream." Just the thought of surrendering the control she had relied on for so long terrified her. Suddenly experiencing a surge of anger, she sat bolt upright and folded her arms defiantly across her chest.

Scott looked over at Alice, who was sitting next to him, with a concerned expression. He then turned to look at Adam and began to speak. "I too appreciated what Ben and Adam shared, and some of what Pastor Jim shared. This has all got me thinking. The whole thing, though, feels like a group therapy session. I told my wife once that I would never participate in something like that, whatever the forum might be." Adam smiled patiently. "Sharing their faith journeys with fellow Christians, as some have done here, along with the inner demons they've dealt with along the way, was a common practice in the early church. It was often done retroactively as part of a faith witness. Peter and Paul both did this, and they did it millennia before the professional discipline of psychology or therapies like analytic psychotherapy and others involving self-actualization existed. Have you considered that some of the most effective aspects of certain contemporary psychotherapies might have naturally occurred in and through the shared experiences of God's loving grace within the early Christian faith community? The New Testament, especially the book of Acts and the Epistles, records the witness of those whose lives were gradually transformed by grace, which helped them integrate some of the deepest and most suppressed and repressed parts of themselves into a more holistic, Christ-centered sense of self. Although the final end here was not just a healthier, better integrated psyche, but spiritual growth and transformation."

Scott had maintained eye contact with Adam and had listened carefully to what he said. "That may be well and good, but all this sharing of a personal nature makes me very uncomfortable." Scott paused briefly and then began to speak with resolve. "Be that as it may, if baring my soul here will help me accomplish whatever I am supposed to do here, I'll give it a go." "Welcome to your first group therapy session, Scott," Ben teased as Scott cast him an irritated look.

"Okay then, as most here have probably gathered, being successful in life has been very important to me. The success I have enjoyed in business, along with the trappings of that success, my large house, the cars, and expensive vacations, for me, attested to that success." Adam looked over at Ben, who was about to make another wisecrack at Scott's expense. He then gently and subtly shook his head not to. "How the heck did he know what I was about to say?" Ben thought to himself. "Of course, none of you know much about my past, and let me say it's what Wes just shared that in part has given me the courage to share what I am about to. My stepfather was incapable of expressing any affection, much less love toward anyone. On top of that,, he was often abusive toward my mother, my sister and me. Suffice it to say he behaved much worse than Wes's father. I never knew my real father. I was a product of a brief affair my mother had before she ever met my stepfather. I could never get my mother to talk about my biological father. All I know is that he was never in the picture as a parent. My half-sister came along later and was the only child my mother and stepfather had together. My stepfather was an alcoholic. He was a big, burly man with a bad temper. He was more verbally than physically abusive. Our mom got the worst of it, but he put her down so much and so often that her self-esteem remained in the gutter until the day she died. He tore us kids down as well. We could do nothing right. I can't ever recall him offering a word of praise to either my sister or me. He was an auto mechanic, but due to his drinking he was only employed sporadically. He was fired from nearly every garage he worked for. Because of his work record, money was always tight. My mother worked as a waitress but the money she brought in only modestly augmented our still meager income. So, if you hadn't guessed by now, I grew up poor. The worst part of it for me wasn't that though, it was that I felt helpless to protect my mother from the abuse my stepfather doled out. My mother, who I dearly loved, was a quiet, gentle soul who loved us unconditionally and showed it in all the ways a mother can. She not only made sure we were fed and clothed but, when we were little, she often held us and comforted us when hurt or just upset." Scott's voice began to crack as he recalled and shared these memories. "I am sorry," he said as he paused for a moment to collect himself. "It's just that these memories bring back some of the hurt I experienced growing up." After a moment or two Scott sat back in his chair and sighed, as if some terrible burden he'd been carrying for a long time had just been lightened. "I don't know if I am at the edge of some cliff with a chasm before me where I must decide whether to leap across it or not, toward God, but I've definitely gotten in touch with some memories and feelings I've ignored or suppressed for a very long time. And as I've been sharing all this, I might as well admit, to myself and you, that none of my success has filled an emptiness I have long felt inside of me. These memories and feelings have surfaced from time to time when I've not been distracted by working to build up my business, or in recent years my church work. My love for my kids used to help fill the void I've felt, and still feel, inside that my successes in life just couldn't. Now that both my son and daughter are in college and out of the house I feel an emptiness inside that I am not sure anything can fill. The superficiality and lack of any deeper meaning in my life has become glaringly apparent to me. Even my relationship with my wife has suffered as we struggle to find something other than material success, and the children to bind us together."

After a short pause Adam started to speak. "Long ago a great Christian wrote, 'My soul is restless until it finds rest in Thee, O Lord.' Perhaps, Scott, this might speak to what you've been feeling." "Perhaps," Scott answered in a resigned but reflective way. Scott then paused momentarily, and looked over at Ben. There was a look of compassion on Scott's face Ben had never seen directed toward him before. "Ben, I owe you a heartfelt apology. I know in our interactions, particularly on the committee, I have treated you disrespectfully. Without fully realizing it or wanting to realize it, I was projecting much repressed anger and hurt I felt in relation to my stepfather onto you. I have long associated alcoholism and alcoholics with abuse, loss of control, and failure. Whenever I hear about or must associate with an alcoholic, it strikes a deep, emotional chord within me. This was something I was repulsed by and never wanted to be associated with. I am just now beginning to see how unfair and destructive this has been to our relationship. Please know if we ever get back to our everyday lives, I will make every effort, with the Lord's help, not to treat you this way anymore." With that Ben quietly nodded in a deeply appreciative way and said, "Thank you."

After a few moments of silence Adam, looking compassionately out at the whole group, said, "A number of you have shared personal life experiences, some of which were painful and traumatic. And even though they are unique and differ from one another, I suspect that, underneath, what you all have in common is an innate desire and need for God's unconditional saving love and healing grace. Once experienced, this in turn engenders a need to gratefully express that love back toward God through the Christ-centered love we share with others. Your lack of trust in the reality and power of that love is evident in your attempts to fill the voids you have felt inside with all the secondary investments that humans tend to make primary, except in your cases they have been within the institutional church.

"Soon the time will come for me to leave you and for those who choose to resume their journeys. Let me say a few more things. It is almost Christmas. For those prayerful Christians empowered by the Spirit to live out their faith passionately, even amid doubts and struggles, and for those who are still seeking such a life, Christmas celebrates the greatest gift ever given to humankind. As you know, long ago a child was born in a cave stable and laid in a manger. A star came to shine overhead to mark the place where He lay. Angels, shepherds in the fields, and wise men arrived to pay homage to this child while Mary kneeled and Joseph stood by the child, gazing upon Him with love and wonder. I think you all know the rest of the story. But the story did not end there. That child grew up and fulfilled a mission culminating in His resurrection and the shedding abroad of his Spirit in the hearts of all those who dare to trust that God's promises are true. The ultimate proof of which is to be found, individually and collectively, in the lives of those who seek to live out their faith as their deepest and greatest passion."

Adam then paused and cast a loving look around the circle. "Ben spoke of feeling like he was at the edge of a chasm, and of a decision each one must make to leap over that chasm. For him this chasm contains all his fears, insecurities, hurts, faith doubts, and pridefulness. By leaping into God's arms, he hopes to no longer deny but trust God with all the chasm represents. This analogy is one way of saying that every individual in the end, even with the empowerment of the Holy Spirit, still has the freedom to pull back from the very edge of that cliff. The decision is always yours. In a cynical world and culture that so often demands empirical proof and verification before encouraging one to put their trust in anything, such a decision is understandably hard, truly impossible without the prayerfully requested assistance of the Holy Spirit.

"The Holy Spirit will guide, empower, inspire, nurture, counsel, and even lead you right to the edge of that cliff and then stand with you, and dwell within you, yet you will still be left free to count the cost and choose that relationship with God and his saving love in Christ. That same Spirit will be with as you leap over whatever yawning chasm you might envision lies between you and your salvation, until you are safe in the arms of God. And while this may not be the last time you leap such a chasm, once truly having made that leap you will have experienced something of the empowering love of God, which, looking back, has the power to reassure you that God's faithfulness and promises are true. God longs to hold each of you in His arms and help you begin a journey where you gradually and more authentically become what you were truly created to be. For those of you who are prayerfully empowered to passionately share your faith, you should not become coercive in how you share that faith, but neither should you deny the core truths of the faith. Simply witness to your faith journey in ways that are appropriate and respectful and be open to the Spirit's ongoing guidance. Strive to meet others where they're at, and not where you are at. For those who follow Jesus out of the church and into the rest of their lives, their faith is their heart's greatest treasure, and they are prayerfully ready to sacrifice whatever pretender to their heart's throne threatens to unseat it. Each of you here today has been created as a potential vessel for God's love to shine through. Wherever you gather with others prayerfully in Christ's name and grace, the light of God's love will be magnified and shine through that faith community into a world where darkness still dwells."

As Adam finished speaking those in the circle facing the fireplace began to see something wondrous. At first, they thought their eyes were deceiving them, for atop the mantel and the white layer of cotton that ran the full length across it, the beautifully carved olive wood nativity pieces appeared to have come to life and be moving. The wise men and shepherds at either end of the mantel suddenly took on the appearance of miniature people and, from either end of the mantel, were moving toward the cave stable at its center, the shepherds with their sheep, and the wise men upon their camels. A collective gasp could be heard from those in the circle facing the fireplace. This drew the attention of the rest, including those with their backs to the fireplace, who quickly turned around. All now shared astonishment at what they were seeing. A second wave of gasps could be heard as a radiant beam of light shone out from the star atop the Christmas tree in the far-right back corner of the tavern. The beam of light streamed toward the fireplace mantel until it came to shine on the cave stable, where it bathed the Christ child in the manger in a warm, glittering, golden light that radiated out enveloping Mary, Joseph, the babe, and the cave stable. As all were fixated on this scene, the child in the manger suddenly seemed to come to life. Moving and extending its arms out, it smiled with an infant's innocence while somehow projecting the majestic gift to the world it embodied. Joseph, who had been standing off to one side of the manger, moved a few steps closer and leaned over the manger in a protective, loving stance. Mary, who had been standing on the other side of the manger, then knelt next to manger, epitomizing the appearance of maternal love. With all transfixed on the unfolding nativity scene, and with the figurines having arrived at their final customary places, they all stopped moving and transformed back into their original carved wooden forms.

Enter Sophia

DISTRACTED AS THEY HAD been by this miraculous unfolding scene that seemed to epitomize the astounding nature of their shared experience at the Inn, they had failed to notice that Adam was no longer with them. Everyone had turned around and looked to Adam for an explanation of what they had just beheld. Exclamations of astonishment could be heard as they realized that he was gone. They then talked among themselves trying to make sense of what they had just seen, while nervously anticipating what might come next. The Staff door suddenly swung open, and Old Pete re-emerged. He greeted them with a smile and jovial hello, and made his way over to them, half sitting upon the center stool in front of the bar's counter. "Soon," he said, "you may choose to journey on. Whoever chooses to remain here may do so, and we will continue to work with you, so that you might be strengthened before renewing your journeys. Shortly someone else will be joining you. Her name is Sophia, and she will be the one to send those of you who choose to journey on, on your way. Take a little time now to reflect on the decision you are about to make, and if helpful discuss it among yourselves. As for me," Old Pete said as he rose from the stool, "my time with you is at an end. I pray that God's blessings be upon you all, and that His Spirit will continue to be with you and guide you on your journey." With those final words Old Pete made his way back to the Staff door, turned, smiled, waved one last time, and exited. Most, still overcome by the successive unfolding events that had just occurred, managed sincere but tentative smiles, waves, and goodbyes. A change had come over all there. Even those who had remained quiet through much or all of the discussion with Adam had listened more attentively to what had been shared in a more receptive and self-effacing way.

Left to themselves, they now waited with a mixture of anticipation and anxiety for what was to come next. Fred, who for once wasn't scowling, was smiling faintly and could be overheard saying to Scott, "I kind of like it here, it feels like a very weird but not entirely unpleasant vacation." Wes turned toward Alice and said, "I've decided to continue the journey. What are you going to do?" Alice slowly unfolded her arms and, grabbing the sides of her chair tightly with both hands until they turned white, said, "I don't like it, they're sending us back out into a bitter winter storm to journey toward God knows where." Wes responded, "Maybe God does know where, Alice. I am not sure, but I think it might be toward a real destination this time, toward God, maybe heaven. I am still not sure if we're alive, or dead, or if this is a dream or hallucination, but the whole thing seems way too real to be either of those. How we got here, and exactly where we are, remains something of a mystery, but what we've been through here, Old Pete, Adam, the discussions are all beginning to make sense. Most of us didn't have a clue as to what it meant to be a Christian. I seriously doubt if we ever considered prayerfully chose to live our faith out with any kind of passion, as if it was the most important thing in our life, our greatest treasure. Perhaps that's the real reason the congregation and our committee members could never find any common ground. We were missing the one thing that could have bonded us together, provided common ground, and offered a common vision, a shared passion for a living relationship with Jesus Christ. I don't have all the answers, heck I now have a whole new set of questions, but I guess I am ready to take that leap Ben was talking about. Do I know if God will catch me or if God's Spirit will be with me before, during, and after, where it might validate my faith amid my everyday life? I don't, Alice. I guess that's why faith, as Pastor Jim taught us, means putting our trust in God's faithfulness, and not just in a set of beliefs, traditions, or an institution. I take this faithfulness to mean that, once gifted with the eyes and ears of faith, I will be better able to recall memories of God's past faithfulness, which, along with the empowerment of the Spirit, give us the strength to journey on.

"And another thing, I may not be book smart, but I figured out what that sign with the Bible verse hanging under the big leather book Old Pete used to introduce us meant. I now understand that Scripture must point beyond itself to the living Christ before its pages can fill our lives with truth and wisdom. For the first time ever I am excited, if I ever get back to Kansas, about reading the Bible more carefully for myself. I used to see the Bible as an ancient religious book full of untrue stories and with little relevance for our times. Most of all I can now see, as Old Pete said, that it was no accident that led me to this place. Whatever and wherever this is, I can now see God's hand at work here.

"Besides all of this, I guess I now just want to live for something deeper, more meaningful, more fulfilling, and that liberates me to be more authentically who I am. The bottom line these days, as Ben said, is you can choose to live for yourself because you doubt everything except the material world around you, or you can choose to live for something greater than yourself and this world, something that can transform your life in and from this world. Atheists can say what they like, but I can't think of anything better to live for, with heart, mind and soul, than a love of God and others as yourself. This, after all, as Pastor Jim reminded us, was Jesus' greatest commandment. I've tried the other path, and it hasn't worked that well for me."

"What about all the horrible things done in the name of religion? That sure has filled me with doubts about the Christian truth," Alice complained. "I am just beginning to understand why this isn't a fair criticism of faith. I think the key words to look at," Wes replied, "are 'in the name of religion.' Just because someone says they're doing something in the name of Christianity doesn't mean they are in any way really a Christian. Any ideology, even patriotism, freedom within the framework of democracy, can be distorted and misused. For that matter, as Ben and Jim said, science itself can as well when no longer content to be a method for arriving at one kind of fact or truth and presents itself as the only truth." "Wow, I am not sure I even know you anymore, Wes," Alice said, shaking her head and sitting back in shock.

"Well, I for one am not ready to trust the people here, or this experience. All this reminds me of what happens to those people who suddenly become super religious. They get that glassy-eyed look, and all of a sudden all they can talk about is how much they love Jesus, and they start carrying a Bible with them everywhere. It's not long before they start trying to impose their religion on others. That's not for me; I am going to stick around here a bit longer, or at least until I wake up from whatever this is." At this point Pastor Jim, who had overheard them talking, looked over at Alice.

"Alice, from what you've shared, I understand you have a need for control, but I don't think opening ourselves to a relationship with the living Christ takes away free will or all control over our lives. Also, I don't think the faith leap Ben was talking about was the kind you just described. What you described was more about a decision to adhere to some black and white religious belief system, often based on some equally black and white interpretation of Scripture, that displaces a more dynamic and unshackled faith life. I've long felt that this puts the transcendent God, who we can only know partly in Jesus Christ, in a box. Really what they're doing has more in common with you, and your need for control. Where they have perhaps semi-consciously used religion for that purpose, you cling to your rational problem-solving skills as the means of maintaining control. What you and they are both missing out on is the mystery, awe, and wonder inherent in a more open-ended faith life that rests securely in God's saving unconditional love and faithfulness, a faithfulness that becomes increasingly clear, despite uncertainties, in a lived out faith life. It must be exhausting to continuously try to adhere, in a narrowly conformist way, to such a self-reliant belief system. I also think such efforts once again fit the description of works righteousness we discussed earlier."

Scott, who had been listening in, then interjected, "I don't think this relates, but I'd still like to share a new insight I've gained. I've always found proselytizing, self-righteous atheists who have zero tolerance for faith or religion annoying. This despite not understanding, up till now, what being a Christian is about. I've read where atheists have compared an experientially time-tested faith, despite the countless lives it has transformed for the better, to a belief in unicorns, fairies, and other fanciful creatures. I want to say I can now see just how inept a comparison this is. If I remember it correctly from my logic course in college, I think it's called a categorical fallacy, faith being a time-tested, lived out truth based on the testimony of actual historical witnesses. The other has come to be seen as pure fantasy without any historical basis. Having shared this and setting it aside if it takes a radical leap to live one's faith, I can't think of a better way to live one's life, as Wes said, than through the saving, empowering grace of Jesus Christ to love God and others. It's certainly better than a life lived just for oneself in an absurd, meaningless universe. Also, given no faith in any ultimate, transcendent truth, most, I would think, would be prone to accepting a relativist hodgepodge of incoherent, foundationless values. Alice, you've reduced God to an external customer service rep who you only call on when confronted with a problem you can't solve.

"I think one thing that we're all being led to understand here, albeit by way of a unique and mysterious crash course, is that merely adhering to religious tradition, much less some lesser institutional tradition, can not stand in for the subjective experience of a lived faith where we claim that truth as our own." Scott suddenly paused, grew quiet for a moment, and then said, "I can't believe I just said all that. I mean, despite what you all might think, I did listen to many of Pastor Jim's sermons and too much of what's been said here, but I've always stopped short of wanting to relate it, even if only metaphorically, to my life. All I felt up to now was a stubborn defiance, a little like you, Alice, born of a desperate need to remain independent and stay in control. Somehow in our time at this inn that resistance has been lowered enough for me to seriously consider what has been said here, particularly about the dangers of substituting externals for a living personal faith, particularly that of belief in belief."

Alice stared at Scott in astonishment and then at the others in the group. "What's happened to you people? I don't know if it's the bread, beer, Old Pete, Adam, or all of the above, but you're certainly not the people who arrived here or who I've known for a long time." Alice had made this remark more in a tone of amazement than resentful anger. Then, pausing briefly and in a more acquiescent tone, she said, "Even if you're right Scott, I am still not ready to go back out there. Exerting control over my life has been all that's allowed me cope for a long time, and I am just not ready to give that up yet." "Well Alice, Adam did say you could stay here and that they're willing to work with whoever chooses to stay behind, so I think you'll still be okay." Scott then added, "And who knows, if this is a miraculous collective dream, maybe I'll see you when we all come out of it, and if Adam and company are who I suspect they are, they would be able to continue working with us back in our everyday lives as well."

Audrey, who had been sitting at the table next to Ben and Lynn near the entrance to the tavern, had muttered in a voice both resentful and defiant, "You can all go if you want, but I won't. If my only option is to remain here for however long, then that's what I choose to do." Ben turned toward Audrey and, for the first time in a sympathetic and understanding way, said, "Audrey, given what you shared earlier, I finally understand where you're coming from. For you God is first and foremost a scary, judgmental, and patriarchal father figure. There was a time when I believed in that sort of God too, but the more I've read and studied the Scriptures, particularly the New Testament, for myself, the more I realized that isn't the God the Gospels are telling us about, the God who came among us as Jesus Christ. If I were you, I too would be afraid to journey toward that God for fear that I would never be accepted for who I really am and wouldn't measure up, no matter how hard I tried to prove myself worthy. I know how hard you've tried, and how much you've resented those who didn't try as hard as you. Just know Lynn and I will be praying for you. Believe me, though, when I tell you that I don't mean this in the self-righteousness, 'I am saved but you're not kind' of way, but as a fellow journeyer who in the past has strayed way off the path, stumbled about, and may yet again.

"What I do know and sense is that you'll be in safe and loving hands here." As Ben was saying this, both Lynn and Ben, who were sitting on either side of Audrey, reached over and grasped her hands, clasped tightly and nervously together in her lap. With her head down she had the pose of someone making a defiant last stand. Audrey then sighed, raised her head in a resigned way, and in an uncharacteristically humble tone said, "If I am truly honest with myself, which I haven't been in a very long time, I must admit, as Ben said, that I am afraid of God's judgment. I guess my God has been pretty one dimensional and Old Testament oriented. Maybe I do need to remain here and process these fears a bit more, before I can journey on. You all go on ahead, I'll be fine here for a time, or for however long they allow me to stay before they kick me out. And just maybe, and I said maybe, I will consider opening myself to a commitment to the kind of relationship with the Lord that some of you talked so convincingly about." "That was, very possibly, a decisive, almost commitment, Audrey," Ben gently teased as he winked at Audrey while wearing a warm, affectionate smile on his face. "And who knows," Audrey mused, "maybe some of us must start further back on our journey toward that relationship. We may first even have to make a commitment to a prayerful pre-journey that leads toward that deeper relationship and commitment." "I couldn't have said it better," Pastor Jim chimed in. "Certainly not shorter," Ben quipped. Casting a fake scowl in Ben's direction. Jim then said, "If I know or have learned anything about God's grace, it's not given out on a first come, first served basis. That's how great God's love is for every one of us. I once heard a wise old pastor say that, while there may be only one main way for those seeking a living relationship with God in Christ, there are as many side paths that lead there as there are pilgrims seeking it."

Audrey, looking over at Lynn and Ben, then lightened the conversations by saying, with a shy smile, "I guess I can be something of a killjoy." "No, not you Audrey," Ben and Lynn said in unison with teasing affection.

These and the other discussions that had been taking place all around the circle suddenly grew quiet as the entry door to the tavern swung open. The wind was whistling and blowing hard as snowflakes settled on the top three or four steps. Footsteps could be heard descending the stairs. A tall figure emerged wearing a heavy overcoat and a red scarf around their neck. Their woolen hat and boots were also red. "This must be the one Adam had talked about," Ben whispered to Lynn, recognizing that, as they unwrapped the scarf from around their neck and removed their hat, it was quite clearly, despite being quite tall, a woman. She had flecks of gray in her otherwise dark hair. She appeared to be in early middle age, although there was an ageless aspect to her face, which had an ethereal, glowing quality to it. She smiled as she looked out over the group staring up at her. Her expression seemed to project wisdom, calm, compassion, and strength all at the same time.

"My name is Sophia," she said breaking through the stunned silence, "and I will both be seeing you on your way as well as guiding each of you on the rest of your journey." Her voice, while calm and soothing, contained something of a wind-driven, whispering quality to it. "How the heck can she do that?" Williard whispered to Scott, "she's only one person." "Shush Williard," Pastor Jim whispered, leaning over toward Williard, adding, "Have a little faith. Try to resist the urge we all have at times in varying degrees to explain everything rationally and in worldly terms. I have a feeling these answers will come in a different way than we're used to. I am coming to see that there are some things, spiritual things, that we won't be able to understand until we are ready to, or are guided to the point where we are capable of understanding them from the inside out. Perhaps some of what we have yet to learn spiritually we're not even equipped yet to know rationally. Such spiritual insights and experiences need not be seen as irrational, but rather non-rational in the sense that our brains and consciousness are not yet capable of grasping the truth they offer. There is more to that scriptural adage that 'God's ways are not always our ways' than we can imagine." Pastor Jim then sat back and thought to himself, "Sometimes I think the enlightenment, with its elevation and eventual deification of reason, also sowed the seeds that eventually would lead to the decline of numerous Christian traditions, at least in the West." He then paused and grew quiet and, despite all he had just said to Williard, he suddenly felt a mild resurgence of his habitual need to have his faith affirmed once more by purely rational arguments.

Despite this, he knew deep down that he would still make the prayerful decision or leap toward a committed, personal faith life. Perhaps what he had just felt was the last gasp of that shadow part of him that sought to assuage his faith doubts and insecurities. It had become a major stumbling block to a genuine faith life, but as with Williard, Jim had grown weary of this ultimately spiritually impotent obsession. Strangely and coincidentally Pastor Jim suddenly recalled the dying words of Saint Thomas Aquinas, one of the most brilliant thinkers and prolific writers in the history of philosophy, Christian theology, and ethics. As he lay dying, Aquinas, recollecting a mystical experience he had had celebrating Mass one year earlier, had said, "Such secrets have been revealed to me that all I have written now appear as so much straw." Then under his breath and speaking to himself, Pastor Jim said, "And maybe, just maybe, the greater proof must come after the leap as we gradually become authentically who we were meant to be, passionately centered in God's love and grace."

Sophia walked along the front of the bar counter, stopped and stood in front of the center bar stool, and began to speak. "Shortly it will be time for most of you to resume your journey. A few of you have chosen to remain behind, and you are welcome to do this with no judgment passed. Just know you are all loved equally by the Innkeeper, and we will continue to work with you." No one at this point even questioned how Sophia could have known that a majority of the group had already decided to journey on, while a few had chosen to remain behind.

Sophia then turned and headed back toward the foot of the stairs. "In a moment I will call out each of your names in turn. As I do so, please come over to me and I will motion for you to ascend the stairs and continue your journey." "If some of you go ahead of me, please wait for me out there. We might as well journey on together from here," Williard suggested cheerfully. Sophia smiled in a gentle, knowing way. "When you leave the inn's tavern, you will find yourself alone on the road outside. God loves each of you as individuals and wants you to come into a relationship with Him/Her that way. Later you will be brought together into a community where you will begin to bond with one another through your shared desire for and experience of that relationship. But for now, each of you must choose to not only journey on but do so on your own." This aroused fears and doubts among the members of the group who had chosen to journey on. They shared the same resurgent anxiety of having to journey on, now alone, down the dark road outside in the midst of a winter storm. Why, they thought, given that at least some of us are on the verge of a leap of faith, must we still face the hazards and uncertainty of this road; why can't we just skip that now and go right to heaven or wake up from whatever this is?

Sophia paused and looked out over those gathered around the circle with compassion. Every set of eyes was upon her. "Trusting the Innkeeper's saving love for you is only the beginning of your renewed journey. It is on this journey itself that He will gradually transform you and help you become all that you can be in that love. This continued journey does not come without risks, hazards, and setbacks. Still, having opened yourself to the reality and truth of His saving grace, your doubts, fears, and any other challenges you may face now have a greater opportunity of being integrated into the authentic individual that the Innkeeper will help you become." "Sophia, if you don't mind me asking one or two more questions," Wes asked timidly. "Why do you keep saying the Innkeeper when for some time now most of us suspect this to be God? And what about Adam and you, who are you both, really? We all have strong suspicions as to who you are, but some affirmation of this might be reassuring before we must resume our journey. Also why haven't we met the Innkeeper, and why couldn't He have been the one to handle everything?" "You're up to three questions, Wes," Ben wise-cracked, causing Wes to give him a disparaging look and tell him to give it a rest. Acknowledging this, Ben said, "I am bad," in a self-deprecating way. Sophia looked at Wes, smiled, and then answered. "This too will become clearer as you journey on. Just know for now that, given the limitations of your mind and senses, the journeys you all must take from here on, first as individuals and later as a community of faith, this is the most helpful way the Innkeeper can be there with you and for you."

Having said this, Sophia looked out quietly on the group again, and with no more questions forthcoming and silence prevailing, she began to call out each name in turn. As each member rose and walked over to Sophia, she extended her arm out and up and toward the door at the top of the stairs, inviting each in turn to ascend the stairs and exit. Surprisingly none of those who chose to journey on hesitated but, accepting the resumption of their journey in a hopeful and trusting, Spirit-filled way, they quietly exited. There was even a rising feeling of excitement and anticipation among them. Pastor Jim was the last one called. When his turn came and he rose to leave, he was the only one to pause and make a remark to Sophia. Turning toward her at the bottom of the stairs, he said simply, "Thank you," and then ascended the stairs and left. Alice, Audrey, and Fred had remained seated. Sophia turned back toward them and said, "We look forward to working with you. Soon after I leave, Old Pete will come out and show you to your rooms."

On the Road Again

THE NEXT THING PASTOR Jim knew, he was walking down the road again. The title of another well-known country song then sprang to mind, "On the Road Again." This he thought, couldn't be mere coincidence. The blizzard had eased into a gentle snowfall. The wind had died down considerably and only an occasional gust could be felt from time to time. Even though he was back on the same road in winter, Pastor Jim no longer felt the hopelessness and despair he had on the road before arriving at the Inn. Something had changed within him. He felt not only hopeful but lighter inside, unburdened of much that had weighed him down for years. He also sensed a presence with him. He did not know if it was Sophia, but it was there just the same, a comforting, assuring, guiding presence. It seemed to be present both within and outside of him. He not only experienced it as a continuing source of empowerment but intuitively sensed he could turn to it prayerfully for counsel and guidance if for any reason he faltered on his way. After Pastor Jim had walked on for some time, he thought to himself, "Despite traveling on alone, and with us all having had the experience at the inn, I do trust that we are all now journeying toward the same wondrous destination." A part of him, though, wondered if he would ever wake up from this journey. All he and the others had heard and learned at the Inn pointed beyond itself toward a closer relationship with God, but where this would be he still wasn't sure. He intuitively knew that this journey and road, for him and the rest, and the fate of those back at the Inn, would not take them directly to be with God. As Pastor Jim continued walking, he uttered a short prayer. "Lord," he prayed, "I am ready, and I am pretty sure most of us are more open to living our lives more centered around a personal relationship with you. Please allow us to return to our lives transformed or at least more open to being transformed by this experience." As he walked on Jim looked up in wonder at the clear night sky, which shone with the lights of thousands of twinkling stars. Suddenly he noticed that one shined brighter than all the rest. Then having caught his eye it appeared to glow even brighter. With his heart racing, Jim watched as a stream of light from the star gradually shone down directly in front of him on the road. It then began to form into the brightest ball of light Pastor Jim had ever seen, brighter than the sun. Strangely, though, it did not hurt his eyes. Intuitively sensing that the light emanated from God, Jim fixated on it with a mix of awe-inspired fear and joyous wonder. At the very center of this circle of light a face appeared; it was that of Adam looking out with love and an accepting compassion upon him. As Adam's face slowly faded back into the light another face gradually began to appear. As it emerged Pastor Jim could see that it was that of a woman, and then as the features became clearly visible, he recognized it as Sophia's. Then as her face slowly faded away the circle of light grew bigger and brighter until it enveloped not only him but the area all around him. Much later Jim found it impossible to find the words to describe to others what he had experienced in the light.

What he could say was that he had felt an unconditional love like he'd never known, a joy like none he could have ever anticipated, and a sense that he belonged and was more at home in that love than he ever could have imagined. As these feelings continued to grow within him, Jim found himself wanting this experience to continue forever. Then as suddenly as it all had begun, the light began to recede and Jim suddenly found himself floating, as before, in a darkness that nevertheless filled him with feelings of calm and peace.

Before he had time to wonder how long this experience would last, he was violently jarred awake, along with all the committee members, by the sound of screeching tires and horns blaring. Screams could be heard from the passengers as they saw the blinding headlights of the rapidly approaching tractor-trailer coming at them head on.

With lightning reflexes, the bus driver swung the wheel hard to the extreme right, as the truck driver, who had momentarily fallen asleep, swerved his truck as hard as he could in the other direction without causing the truck to flip over. By pure luck, or some miracle, the bus and truck managed to swerve out of each other's way without colliding. The truck had gone into a skid, its cab ending up just shy of the ditch on the side of the road in a near upright V formation, and its trailer blocking the lane it had just been in. The bus had gone into a skid too. Passing the truck on the right, it ended up stretching horizontally across its own lane, with its tail end barely missing that of the truck, its front end facing the very edge of the roadside. Fortunately given the route they were on and due to the mid-evening hour, there had been no oncoming traffic. A collective sigh of relief could be heard, with some muttering, "That was about as close as it gets." The bus driver stood up and turned to face the passengers. "Is everyone all right?" he called out. "We're okay, what the heck just happened?" "I am guessing the truck driver fell asleep and crossed the median." A knock on the door turned out to be the truck driver, who confirmed that this was indeed what had happened. After the truck driver apologized profusely and promised to stop and rest, he and the bus driver agreed to go their separate ways as there had been no contact or damage to either vehicle. What Pastor Jim would only find out later, which seemed to him at the time like a strange and unlikely coincidence, was that everyone on the bus had been asleep and all had been violently jarred awake by the sounds of the near-deadly collision. What Jim was to have confirmed by the group a short time later made this coincidence seem like nothing by comparison and could not be explained in any other way but as a miracle of a kind he never could have imagined before their experience at the Inn. They were soon to learn that all on board had indeed had the same shared dream, or whatever it was, albeit from their own personal perspectives.

At the Retreat Center

THE BUS TURNED BACK onto the road and resumed its journey. Adrenaline-fueled chatter over the near-fatal collision could be heard throughout the bus. As nerves slowly calmed, and with an hour or two to go before they would reach the retreat center, all on the bus slowly grew quiet. Before long the hum of the bus's engine was all that could be heard. The lights of the former convent, now retreat center, soon came into view. An expansive manicured lawn and a macadamized parking lot fronted the large, two-story red brick former convent. A four-sided, apex-shaped structure formed a large portion of the roof over the center of the building. Jim soon discovered that this central two-story open area, which extended beyond the back of the building and doubled as a reception area, was the chapel.

The brakes of the bus squealed as it came to a stop in front of the main entrance. A woman wearing ordinary clothing, who all took to be a nun, came out of one of the two large, varnished wooden front doors and through a white columned portico. She then walked briskly toward the bus to greet the new arrivals. Standing at the bus's door she welcomed each passenger in turn as they exited the bus. Once all were grouped together outside the bus she led them toward the entrance to the retreat center. Jim had a few moments to take in the full scope of the building. He noticed that the one-story extensions on either side of the center of the building ended in two large, rectangular, two-story attached structures that were wider than the extensions themselves. Jim would later learn that the dining hall was on the lower level of the rectangular structure at the far-left end of the building.

Soon all were directed past a hallway and into the large, circular room that served as the chapel. Its ceiling was the apex he had sighted outside.

Movable chairs had been piled up and moved to one side. Tables had been set up with plates of cookies and hot chocolate set out for the weary travelers. As Pastor Jim and the others ate the cookies and sipped the hot chocolate, they had a chance to look around the spacious room. They were struck by how conducive it was for spiritual reflection. Beautiful modern stained-glass windows that stretched from floor to the ceiling's edge covered most of the semicircular back side of the room. One of these windows, on the right hand back side, depicted a nativity scene of Mary, Joseph, and the Christ child. A beautiful wooden altar on wheels had been moved from the center of the room to one side near a piano. A rich, red carpet covered the floor. The ceiling of the room was covered by long, wide, varnished light-brown wooden boards, which came together in the top center of the room to form the apex. Candles that sat in holders wrapped in green garlands had been placed in the center of the two tables. This together with the seasonal paper tablecloths reminded all that Christmas was near. Several nuns busied themselves about the large room with various tasks. The committee members were all gathered in the center of the chapel on either side of the tables. Animated chatter filled the room. Standing just off to one side, Jim could not hear clearly what they were saying. Intuitively, though, he could tell by their excited tone, and despite their being tired and the late hour, it was about the near collision a short time before. Jim had first become aware of the shared nature of their experience as he listened to the adrenaline driven talk on the bus that followed the near collision. As they continued to share with one another, each from a subjective perspective, the astounding reality that this was indeed a shared experience became increasingly apparent. Alice and Audrey had shared their experiences as well but with a key difference. While grateful to have found themselves back on the bus, they shared their joint realization that, while they were not yet ready to make a serious commitment to a living faith, they knew their former motivations for serving the church no longer made sense to them. Fred remained largely silent, keeping his thoughts to himself, but the scowl was gone, and with head lowered and wearing a faint, congenial smile he seemed to project a newfound humility. While he did not converse much, he interacted with the others with a friendlier demeanor. Pastor Jim, trying to process all that had happened, had been standing just to the right and behind the gathered committee members. He was still holding a Styrofoam cup of hot chocolate in one hand when he was approached by one of the nuns. Pastor Jim nodded his head in agreement with her suggestion that as soon as the group was finished with their refreshments they all would be escorted to their rooms.

Jim waited until the talk died down and everyone was finished with their refreshments. He then walked toward the group gathered around the tables and began to speak. "We could probably stay awake all night talking about what happened earlier this evening, but despite how excited you still are it might be wise if we retired for the night. The nuns will show you to your rooms. If you have trouble falling asleep or staying asleep, may I suggest you turn our mysterious shared experience this night, as I plan to do, over to the Lord in prayer. Might I also suggest as you do so you reflect prayerfully on what insights you might have gained from a personal perspective. Some rest and further reflection will help deepen and enrich our discussions during this retreat. I for one know that it will be hard to stay asleep, much less go to sleep, given all that's happened, so I know I will be doing some praying and reflecting." "Thanks Pastor," Ben said as the rest looked on, nodding in agreement. "Given our experience earlier tonight, I think this would be a great alternative use of our time." "Well," Jim said in response, "undoubtedly some of us, or all of us, will be tired in the morning, but with the help of a good breakfast the nuns will provide, and of course some extra cups of coffee, I suspect we'll all be very invested in this retreat from here on." "You can say that again," Lynn quipped as the rest once more nodded their heads in agreement. Pastor Jim then offered up a prayer thanking the Lord both for their safe arrival and petitioning the Holy Spirit's discerning guidance and empowerment regarding the wondrous and miraculous experiences they had had that night. He also prayed that they remain open to the ways it might deepen and enrich both their individual and collective faith lives. After all echoed Jim's amen, the group broke up and, escorted by the nuns, trundled off to their separate rooms.

The next morning, after a hearty breakfast, most of the committee members did indeed drink more coffee than usual. After breakfast a nun directed them down the hallway to the rectangular structure at the far right end of the building. This took them into a large meeting area. Floor to ceiling wood-framed windows at the back of the room allowed the morning sun to stream into the inviting space. A beautifully landscaped lawn, which slanted down toward a lake, could be seen through the windows. Small wooden chalet enclosures mounted on poles led down to the lake. Audrey, upon spying them and not knowing what they were, innocently inquired of the nun present, "What's up with all the bird feeders?" The nun, though momentarily taken aback, quickly regained her composure and, smiling patiently and graciously, explained that they were stations of the cross. On the mid outer wall of the room was a large stone fireplace with a wooden mantel. One long couch and two shorter couches with two easy chairs at an angle on either side of the long couch had been positioned in front of the fireplace. They formed a large semicircle around the large stone fireplace within which a well-tended fire flickered and crackled. The nun, with the help of a couple committee members, had brought folding chairs from the fellowship/worship room in case they were needed. The two smaller end couches had been pulled back a bit to make room for them. After the nun had invited everyone to be seated, Pastor Jim sat in one of the easy chairs. Most had brought cups of coffee with them. As they took their seats and settled down, it was apparent that the group exhibited a very different attitude to the one they had before their experience at the Inn. Whatever preliminary reflections some, or all, had had the night before also helped foster a quieter, more thoughtful mindset. Pastor Jim could detect in their quieter demeanor and body language a newfound humility and, he hoped, open-mindedness to a radically different kind of retreat than the one he had anticipated with so much apprehension.

Pastor Jim then asked all to bow their heads in prayer, which they did with surprising reverence. Given his past experiences at committee meetings, at the retreat he had planned to keep the opening prayer and devotion as brief as possible. The only change he had made from the previous night was to the Scripture reading preceding the devotion. This he had changed to John 5:39, recalling the verse on the plaque hanging just below the large leather-bound book at the corner of the bar counter at the inn: "You study the Scriptures diligently because you think that in them you have eternal life. These are the very Scriptures that testify about Me." Although he had second thoughts about the necessity of this verse given the group's transformation. They no longer needed to be challenged by and reflect on this verse, as much as to be more fruitfully open to sharing about how they resonated with its deeper import. When Pastor Jim had called for prayer, there had also been an air of expectancy he had never encountered from the group before. He no longer had to worry that his attempt at setting a spiritual tone would be met with a wisecrack and a business-as-usual mindset. Jim thanked the Lord for the extraordinary, miraculous experience they had all had, and then asked for the Holy Spirit's guidance as they did some soul searching for the deeper, further meaning and purpose that experience might afford their lives individually, as a committee, and for the greater faith community. He finished the prayer by invoking the presence of the Holy Spirit, as a vibrant memory of Sophia came to mind. Then after allowing for a long, pregnant pause, he looked at all those seated around the fireplace and asked the first question of the retreat, the one that would establish the theme and help put the rest of the retreat's format into a finer focus, a format that had remained the same, but to which a radically transformed attitude was now being brought to bear. That question very simply was: "So let me ask each of you in turn, what does it mean to you personally when you say that you are a Christian?"

Christmas Eve

THE CHRISTMAS EVE SERVICE that year as usual was filled to capacity, with standing room only in the back of the sanctuary. The governing committee members were all present and accounted for. They had all agreed to wait until after the New Year to decide on how and with whom they should best share, if at all, their experience at the Inn. When Pastor Jim had asked them if it would be okay to use something of the experience as a sermon illustration on Christmas Eve, they had all been okay with this as long as it was presented as a fictional illustration. Only close family members or the very observant would have detected the subtle changes that had come over most of the governing committee members scattered about the sanctuary pews. Several now sang with considerably more feeling and exuberance. A majority followed the liturgy and said the prayers more fervently, as if imbued with a greater meaning and purpose. For most of the members their faith journey had only begun to take them down a very different road. Even Fred, Alice, and Audrey, who had chosen to remain behind at the Inn, appeared more enlivened than usual, even factoring in that it was a Christmas Eve service. Alice appeared slightly embarrassed when, for the first time during any service, she reached for the Bible in the pew holder in front of her. The first Scripture reading was taken from John 1:1–3. The second from Matthew 2:1–3 concerning the wise men. The third, from Luke 2:1–20, detailed the nativity scene and included the shepherd narrative.

Fred, who was now sitting with his wife, had for the first time that any could recall tried to cast a congenial smile toward those he greeted prior to the worship service. This appeared to be painful for him and involved unpracticed facial muscles that heretofore had rested comfortably in the well-defined, deeply grooved wrinkles of his perpetual scowl. When the children's choir sang "Silent Night" his rather strained expression, which looked more like a painful grimace, uninhibitedly broke free into a wide-mouthed smile stretching those muscles dangerously beyond any previous limit. Others also noticed him exhibiting a certain spontaneity they hadn't seen before when he clapped exuberantly as the children's choir finished singing. Alice, Fred, and Audrey's faith journeys might not have taken them down a different road, but it was very likely that they had arrived at a critical crossroads.

Pastor Jim kept his sermon that night, more of a homily, as brief as possible prior to utilizing their experience as both an extended fictional illustration and conclusion. The sermon's introduction had suggested that not only the wise men, and all there tonight, but anyone who truly encounters the Christ child can be transformed, causing their return journey to take them a different way home. "Unlike the wise men, who literally went a different way home, the road we take back into our homes and lives may at first appear to be the same, but is in fact a very different one. We too can be transformed by this encounter as we come to know more fully who Christ is and why he was born among us." The sermon's introduction also contained a caution. "Most of us here tonight have heard and read the nativity narratives so many times that there is a danger of it being seen as rote Scripture lessons devoid of any deeper meaning or numinous Divine quality. It might be good, then, if I do a reframing and retelling of that story within the larger framework of a different story, context, and set of circumstances. This may afford us a fresh new look at that first Christmas story we know so well."

Allowing for a dramatic pause Pastor Jim began the illustration with these words: "Imagine yourself caught up in an unusually vivid dream. You're walking down a desolate country road amid a growing winter storm. Already unsettled, you soon begin to fear that this journey you have mysteriously found yourself on lacks any ultimate meaning and direction. Then as the storm slowly transforms into a raging blizzard, you're brought face to face with the stark reality of your mortality and the aimlessness of this journey. In a prayer of desperation, you cry out to the Lord to save you. This is a road we will all find ourselves on at some point as the storms of life threaten to overwhelm us, or the desolation, meaninglessness and unfulfilling superficiality of our existence becomes glaringly apparent, inevitably leading to an under-riding despair, world weariness, and a deep longing for something more, even if we're not sure what that is. Many of us who had previously clung to a vestige, or merely the shell of faith we call religion, may well utter that same prayer of desperation.

"But I digress. Suddenly the warm lights of an Inn appear on the side of the road, offering warmth and salvation. Upon entering, you are heartily welcomed by the patrons, all of whom seem to know you and appear equally grateful to have found this place in the middle of nowhere that offered refuge from the raging winter storm. The cozy atmosphere of the Inn's tavern, replete with Christmas greenery and candles wrapped with green ribbon, is a warm, welcoming sight. What most catches your eye, though, is the long bed of white cotton laid across the fireplace mantel below which is a roaring, crackling fire. Upon the cotton, the beautifully carved wooden pieces of a nativity scene have been laid out. Mary, Joseph and the babe in the manger had been placed in the cave stable. Other wooden figurines, the shepherds and their sheep, and the wise men astride their camels approach from either side of the wooden nativity stable. There is a numinous glow to all the figures but especially to the Christ child lying in the manger. After taking a seat at one of the tables, you are drawn back again and again to the figure of the Christ child. As you fix your gaze on the child with its arms outstretched and an infant's innocence and vulnerability, you suddenly experience an overwhelming love, grace, and total acceptance extended to you. You are filled with wonder and an irrepressible desire to know who this child is, will be, and what that might mean for your life. While not having seriously considered this before, you now intuitively know that if you ever wake up from whatever this is, and go back to your everyday reality, you will need the guidance of the Holy Spirit, those filled with that Spirit, and God's word as you seek answers to these questions. In the meantime, the Innkeeper's staff offers you rest, refreshment, and guidance so that you may renew your journey with a newly awakened, exhilarating sense of direction and purpose.

"Some who have entered God's Inn tonight that we call the church have found themselves in the midst of a growing winter storm, with all manner of trouble from illness and failure to deep insecurities along with the guilt and shame and anxiety they spawn within us. Imagine this like a relentless winter storm to be increasingly swirling about you. Perhaps some part of you tonight, without being fully aware of it, is hoping that this story you've heard so many times over the years will instill in you something of the true spirit of Christmas. Perhaps the story will also evoke some reflection. 'Could the ultimate reality we call God,' you dare ask yourself, 'really have come among us that first Christmas Eve? Could it really have been God's plan to build a bridge of love from us back to Him/Her through the later sacrifice and resurrection of that child?' Then for a moment an old doubt surfaces. 'Why,' you ask yourself, 'would that ultimate Being/reality we call God bother themself with such an insignificant creation, even if it does contain a spark of the Divine within?' But then, perhaps due to the ambience and inspiration of the evening, for the first time it occurs to you, just maybe it is the very inestimable power, wisdom, and love of God that made it possible for Him/Her to be born, both fully human and Divine, among such a seemingly insignificant creature, in the humblest of circumstances. Perhaps only God whose essential nature is an unfathomable love would have had the inestimable power to manifest itself to us in a way that defies human understanding.

"Now let us return to the traditional narrative of that first Christmas Eve. I want you to imagine that you are there that first Christmas Eve. Imagine yourself descending from a nearby hillside toward that cave stable. A brilliant star overhead clearly illuminates the entire unfolding nativity scene below. You soon arrive before the stable itself and peer within. There is something special about what you are witnessing. You can't articulate it at first, but it fills you with awe and reignites the dying embers of your faith. You open yourself to the otherworldly presence that surrounds and envelops the greater nativity scene that first Christmas Eve: the star; Mary, Joseph, and the babe; the wise men and shepherds; even the animals all seem to glow with a luminosity invoked by a Divine presence on a night where heaven and earth met to bestow God's greatest gift to humankind, God's grace and love incarnate. Of course, Christ's Spirit may seek to be born into your life in any set of circumstances where you experience Christ as uniquely present, as if for the first time. However it might happen, it is an experience that seems more real, more filled with love and grace than anything you've experienced before. Suddenly you are faced with a decision, Do I allow the Christ child to live and grow within me, in heart, mind, and soul when I leave this place, or do I back away from this experience and resume the ultimately meaningless and pointless journey that brought me here? This is a decision everyone must make for themselves as individuals, often more than once. However, having once experienced Christ's Spirit being born within us, we are much less apt, ever again, to reduce what being a Christian means to some abstract, dogmatic, institutional, or superficial religious understanding. In short, it worked. However imperfectly, we can feel ourselves beginning to be transformed from the inside out as we allow our relationship with Christ's Spirit to grow within us. In the wake of the growing light of faith within, our recollections of God's past faithfulness reassure, renew, and, if need be, open us for the first time to a relational commitment to God in Jesus Christ. It is a deeply personal decision that requires, in part, a consistent, confessional prayer life, lest we back away from that grace and fall back into obsessions with the worldly pursuits we had substituted for a relationship with the living God through our Savior Jesus Christ. The first leads back out into the raging storm; the other, at first, may seem to lead back out to the same road and swirling storm of trials and tribulations. But the road is not the same. Now, despite facing many or all of the same challenges, something is different. You soon feel like you are journeying toward a brighter, clearer future filled with hope, meaning, and purpose. Moreover, you now can prayerfully avail yourself of the light of God's saving love to guide you toward your true destination and eternal home. My prayer for all of you here tonight is that when you truly encounter the Christ child, be it on a Christmas Eve or at any other time and place, that you take Him with you in your heart, mind and soul, and allow Him to grow up and fulfill His mission in and through you, and through all those that journey together in His name.

"The proof that so many non-believers demand cannot be given in a worldly way, but in the otherworldly way we lead lives transformed by the light of Christ's love, a light magnified wherever Christians truly gather, prayerfully, in Christ's name to love God and one another."

www.ingramcontent.com/pod-product-compliance
Lightning Source LLC
Chambersburg PA
CBHW070602180626
46817CB00005B/1954